Captive Down Under

A Story of Imprisonment and Hope

by Giulio Zambon

ISBN: 978-0-6451827-0-5

Introduction

Captive Down Under tells the story of Lieutenant Rosario Roccafiorita, an Italian officer who, after being captured in Lybia in 1941, was kept in Palestine for some months before being sent to Australia, where he was held till 1947.

While this is a work of fiction and all its characters, including the protagonist, Rosario Roccafiorita, are invented, the events that those characters experience are based as much as possible on what happened to real-life counterparts. And all the locations and the major historical figures in the background are real.

On 10 June 1940, Italy entered WWII on the side of Germany. During the course of the War, Great Britain and their allies captured approximately 600,000 Italian troops, who were then sent to POW camps all over the world, including Australia. (1)

In May 1941, the Queen Mary, which had been converted to troop transport, carried the first 2,000 Italian POWs to Australia and among them was Roccafiorita.

Between 1941 and 1943, Australia received custody of more than 18,400 Italian POWs. After September 1943, when Italy signed an armistice with the Allies, the Australian government, following the lead of the British, instead of freeing the Italian POWs, sent many of them to work on farms. It is estimated that more than 13,000 Italian prisoners held in Australia worked on farms with very limited military supervision. Officers were exempt, but Rosario volunteered, both to avoid being enclosed by barbed-wire fences and to leave behind the violent conflicts between die-hard Fascists, still loyal to Mussolini, and the Royalists like himself. (2)

I wrote Captive Down Under as part of my PhD thesis at the University of Canberra and I still have a web version of it that shows all notes and abbreviations as pop-ups and lets you jump to an appendix and back to the main text by clicking the mouse. But I'm not sure I will ever be able to publish it in that form.

You will find that, unlike most works of fiction, *Captive Down Under* includes a lot of notes. To make them as little intrusive as possible and let you enjoy reading the story without interruptions, I grouped together all the notes belonging to the same paragraph, placed them at the each of each chapter, and wrote the notes and their markers in grey. I also included several appendices to limit the saize of the notes.

At the end of the book you will also find a complete list of all the abbreviations I used, including, for completeness, some that you will probably find pretty obvious

I hope you will enjoy *Captive Down Under* and welcome any comment you might have. My email address is giulio@zambon.com.au.

Canberra, 27 May 2021.

1. You can read the full declaration of war in Appendix A. Mussolini made the most important announcements from the balcony of Palazzo Venezia. Besides the declaration of war, perhaps the most famous of those speeches was the proclamation of the Empire, made on 9 May 1936, as reported by the Argus of Melbourne on the 11th (reproduced in Appendix B). The newspaper only reports parts of Mussolini's speech, but it is very interesting. The original audio recording of the speech (in Italian) is on YouTube. The translation of the full speech is available in Appendix C.

2. The Army Directorate of Prisoners of War and Internees reported in 1951 that a total of 18,432 Italian POWs were held in Australia between 28 May 1941 and 12 February 1945, but that number, universally accepted as valid, might not be correct. That total exceeds by 12 the sum of the detailed numbers provided elsewhere in the same report (pp 101, 103, and 105). Furthermore, with my own research, I have been able to identify 18,425 Italians among the list of 44,513 POWs and internees made available by the NAA. My results are still preliminary and I will need to perform additional checks before being able to release them.

   The official report of the Directorate of Prisoners of War and Internees at Army Headquarters indicates that the total number of POWs employed in Australia was approximately 13,167 (see Appendix D for the details).

Rome – Monday 10 June 1940, late afternoon

Excerpts from Mussolini's announcement that Italy has declared war on Britain and France. (1)

Fighters of the land, sea, and air! Blackshirts of the revolution and of the legions! Men and women of Italy, the Empire and the Kingdom of Albania! Hearken! (2)

A fateful hour tolls in the sky of our fatherland (enthusiastic cheers). This is the hour of the irrevocable decisions. The declaration of war has already been delivered (cheers, loud cries of "War! War!") to the ambassadors of Great Britain and France. We take the field against the plutocratic and reactionary democracies of the West, which have always hindered the march, and often threatened the very existence, of the Italian people. (3)

[...]

Italy, proletarian and fascist, is for the third time standing, strong, proud, and united as never before (the crowd screams with one voice: "Yes!"). There exists only one word categorical and binding for everyone. It already flies across and inflames the hearts from the Alps to the Indian Ocean: Victory! (The people burst forth in high acclaim) And we will win, to finally give a long period of peace and justice to Italy, to Europe, and to the world.

1. I couldn't find the exact time, but it must have been late afternoon, because if you watch the speech on YouTube you will notice that the shadows in Piazza Venezia were quite long.

Benito Mussolini was the Italian prime minister from 23 March 1923 to 29 July 1943. He liked to be called "Duce", an old-fashion Italian word derived from the Latin Dux, which means "guide". But, in reality, he established a totalitarian regime based on violence and the suppression of civil liberties. Mussolini's regime inspired Hitler, who, ten years later, chose to be called "Führer", which in German means "guide". The Wikipedia page about Mussolini provides a good starting point for exploring the dictator's life.

2. The Blackshirts (Italian: camicie nere, CCNN, or squadristi) were fascist paramilitary armed squads in Italy during the period immediately following World War I and until the end of WWII. Blackshirts were officially known as the Voluntary Militia for National Security (Milizia Volontaria per la Sicurezza Nazionale, or MVSN).

Mussolini adopted terms like Dux and legion to present his modern dictatorship as a revived Roman Empire. This was also reflected in his obsession with imperial symbols like the eagle and the fasces. During the late Roman Empire, the Dux was the general in charge of several legions. But Duce, the Italian equivalent of Dux, meant "guide", and Mussolini liked to fashion himself as somebody who would lead Italy to "her rightful place" among the most successful and powerful European nations. The legions were the elite units of the Roman army and consisted entirely of Roman citizens. Up to five thousand men strong, the legions were numerically equivalent to modern brigades. The eagle was the standard of Roman legions and became a symbol of the power of Imperial Rome. Fasces are bundles of wooden rods with an axe. Originally an Etruscan symbol of power, it was adopted by the Romans. They gave the name to the Fascist party.

When Italy invaded and occupied Ethiopia in 1935, the King of Italy assumed the title of Emperor. Then, in April 1939 Italy occupied and annexed Albania.

3. Fateful is a word typical of Mussolini's rhetorical lexicon. According to Ledeen, "Virtually the entire ritual of Fascist politics made familiar by Mussolini – the balcony address, the Roman salute, the dramatic dialogues with the crowd, the use of religious symbols in a new secular setting – was influenced by [the Italian poet Gabriele] D'Annunzio".

Since the end of WWII, most Italians have distanced themselves from Fascism. But up to 1941, when the war seemed to be the winning blitz Mussolini had promised, he had a lot of supporters.

Bardia – Thursday 2 January, 1941, evening (1)

Cara Mamma, I am writing to you in my diary because there would be no point in sending a letter. All correspondence is censored and what I would like to tell you would never get through. (2)

The enemy constantly harasses our posts with sorties and sniper shots. They are softening us up. Soon they will attack in force. There is no doubt about it. A few weeks ago, they re-took Sidi Barrani, some 120 km to the east, which we had conquered in September. Bardia will be next. (3)

My post is almost two kilometres behind the barbed wire. The enemy snipers cannot reach us. We only need to be watchful when we hear an aeroplane flying overhead. They usually fly quickly across. But sometimes, perhaps when our anti-aircraft guns are slow to react, they come lower and try their luck with the machine guns. Fortunately, so far, none of my men has been hit.

I command a section of 75/27 field cannons. This will not tell you anything, I know. But hopefully, when the war is over and you read this letter, I will be beside you to explain everything. I like to think so. I imagine us sitting in the shade of the Saracen olive tree behind the barn, with a glass of lemonade, at peace with the whole world. (4)

I wish our commanders took a more aggressive approach. Instead of sending out patrols to raid enemy posts and pester them in any way we can, they keep us sitting tight behind our barbed wire and anti-tank ditches, like a turtle with head and legs pulled in. All we do is battle against lice and fleas. (5)

Although I haven't yet fired a single shot, I already hate this war. I swore allegiance to the King to defend our country, not to be the aggressor in a war started by a "maestro" with delusions of grandeur. (6)

I still remember Mrs Hollingberry and her afternoon teas. And her husband, with his funny handlebar moustache that he kept stroking. Are those the people we are fighting against? Is their son Charles on the other side of the barbed wire? We spent so many afternoons riding together across the fields. Are we now going to shoot at each other? (7)

I only hope that when the British will finally make their move, I will be able to do my duty with honour. All soldiers who have never been in battle fear that they will freeze or, worse, run away. Until you actually face the enemy, you don't know whether you will be a hero or a coward. (8)

Lieutenant Roccafiorita reflected for a moment. Then he closed the small book he had been writing in, screwed the cap onto the pen, and packed both into a bag made of oilcloth. This he slid into the left pocket of his sahariana jacket. He extinguished the smelly tallow candle and wrapped himself tight in his greatcoat, pulling a blanket on top of himself to ward off the chill of the night. (9)

Before closing his eyes, Roccafiorita looked at the sky. The absence of the moon made it easier to identify the group of stars that his grandfather called The Three Merchants, and above it the Pleiades, his favourite constellation. Comforted by the familiar sight, he fell asleep almost immediately. (10)

It was not going to be a long rest. The British, taking advantage of darkness, had been moving troops into position for an attack before dawn. On paper, the Italian fortifications looked formidable, with more than eighty sheltered defence posts, two 29-km fences of barbed wire, anti-tank ditches, and land mines. But the Italian commander, expecting an attack from the south, had weakened the northern part of the defence perimeter and, to compound that problem, had not designated any quick-response unit to move freely in the rear.

The British, recognising the shortcomings of the Italian defences, attacked from the north.

Roccafiorita was shocked into wakefulness by a series of powerful explosions. His men were already running to their posts, but all they could do was look at the flashes and listen to the detonations. This was the British Navy pounding the Italian fortress from their positions off the coast, while the Italian Navy was nowhere to be seen. A few minutes later, the night was turned into day, when enemy planes dropped dozens of parachuted flares. Then wave after wave of enemy planes added their bombs to the naval shells, turning the land into an inferno of fire and dust. (11)

Roccafiorita's men slammed the heavy breeches of the cannons into position and waited for the order to fire, but the enemy was not in sight. Minutes passed and the frustration among them grew. Some coped by chewing on one cigarette after another; others kept checking and rechecking the shells neatly piled around them. When the field telephone rang, Roccafiorita grabbed it with such strength that the knuckles of his left hand cracked. It was the arty spotter on the hill north of their location. Enemy troops were advancing through the valley below. They finally had a target. (12)

All the pieces of the battery moved as if connected to one another, their barrels turning and lifting towards an enemy they couldn't see. And then, Roccafiorita shouted "Fuoco a volontà" (fire at will), and, to use a fitting cliché, all hell broke loose.

Load, ready, fire; load, ready, fire; load, ready, fire. How many shells had they already spent? The men worked like machines the whole morning, their bare torsos sleek with sweat, waiting for enemy troops to appear, at once yearning to fight and hoping that it would not happen, that the first lines of defence would drive the enemy back.

At noon, Roccafiorita ordered cease fire and walked from post to post, wading through clouds of burned gun powder and cordite. The persistent ringing in everybody's ears forced him to shout in order to exchange a few words with his men. A few minutes later, foreign troops were spotted as a dense cloud of dust and smoke coming in from the north, and the Italian gunners finally had a visible target, which they pounded on with all they had. Another artillery post less than a kilometre to the east concentrated its fire on the same target and the enemy, hammered from two directions, was forced to take shelter in a dry riverbed.

But soon, despite the shells falling among their ranks, the enemy troops resumed their advance. They spread out an 800-metre front to reduce the effectiveness of cannon shelling, and came forward. Less than one hour later, the cannons fell silent, and the gunners had to fight at close quarters for their own lives.

After emptying his handgun, Roccafiorita threw it against an advancing enemy soldier and jumped on him, his teeth bared. They fell together to the ground. Roccafiorita brought his right arm back to deliver a punch, but he never completed the action. Another enemy used the butt of his rifle to hit Roccafiorita on the back of the head, and the lieutenant dropped to the ground with a long sigh. (13)

His last thought, before succumbing to darkness, was "Perhaps not a hero, but not a coward either".

When he regained consciousness, his senses came back one after the other, as if to give him time to fully appreciate what they were telling him. First, the acrid smell of cordite, mixed with the sweet smell of blood and the ever-present reek of unwashed bodies. Then came the taste of dust and the sensation of grit between his teeth, followed by the dumb ache of his muscles and the throbbing in his head.

He became aware that somebody was shouting very close to his face. "Signor Tenente, Signor Tenente!" Spittle was hitting his nose and cheeks.

Roccafiorita opened his eyes and, for a moment, thought that he had died and that the devil had come to claim his soul. The face before him couldn't have possibly belonged to a man. It was a black mask of grime, with bloodshot eyes bulging out as if they were about to explode. The lieutenant blinked a few times before realising that he was looking at the bearded face of Corporal Pol. He suddenly became aware of the sound of far explosions and of moaning nearby. (14)

"Signor Tenente, are you OK?"

When he replied, Roccafiorita's voice came out like a croak.

"Yes, yes, I'm fine. Now get off me, will you? Or have you already forgotten what a woman looks like and have decided to try your luck with me?"

The corporal rolled to the side with a grin. As long as the lieutenant kept his sense of humour, the world was still in order.

Roccafiorita pushed himself up to a seated position with a grimace of pain. Around him, guarded by three enemy soldiers, were the survivors of his group: a dozen men sitting on the ground, their eyes downcast. A few metres away, twice as many Italian and British soldiers lay in the dirt side by side, some groaning or feebly asking for help, others completely still, their eyes staring at a sky they could no longer see. A medic was carefully stepping between the prone soldiers, kneeling down to examine them, administering injections to reduce their suffering.

The sun was setting when a British sergeant shouted in heavily accented Italian that they should form half a dozen queues. Under the watchful eyes of three soldiers with their rifles at the ready, they were given water for their canteens and dry Italian rations.

When Roccafiorita reached the front of his queue, he asked in English, "Can I have a cigarette?"

The corporal who was distributing the rations looked at him for a moment as if he had heard a horse sing opera and then, turning his head to the left, shouted "Hey, sarge, we've got an Itie here who speaks English." He handed Roccafiorita a ration, set on top of it two crumpled cigarettes he took from the front pocket of his uniform, and said, "Wait here to the side for the sergeant". Then, craning his neck to look around Roccafiorita, he called, "Next!"

Roccafiorita had already noticed that the British soldiers were often taller than the average Italian. With his 175 cm of height, he was considered in Italy to be a tall man, but he had already seen several enemy soldiers who were at least 10 cm taller than him. The sergeant approaching him at a slow and measured pace was not one of those, though. He was rather short and stocky, with a neck that could have belonged to a boxer or a wrestler. (15)

"You the one who speaks English?" the sergeant asked without any preamble.

"Yes, I am," replied Roccafiorita without volunteering any further information.

"How come?"

"I learned it."

The sergeant studied him for a few second before replying.

"Look, here, lieutenant. I understand that we are enemies and all that, but you were the one who started this mess. If there is anyone who should be cross it's me, right?"

Roccafiorita suddenly burst out laughing. "You don't sound like the British I know!"

The sergeant lips curved slightly upward. "I'm sort-of British alright, but of the type you find on the other side of the world."

"You are Australian."

"Sergeant Graeme McHugh, 2nd Australian Infantry Division, 7th Battalion, A Company," replied the sergeant offering his hand. (16)

Roccafiorita returned the sergeant's firm shake. "Lieutenant Rosario Roccafiorita, 63rd Cyrene Division, 45th Artillery Regiment, 2nd Battery."

"Were you commanding this post?"

"Yes, I was," said Roccafiorita; and then, after a short pause, "And I lost it".

"You almost forced us to turn back," said the sergeant with a note of respect in his voice. "If all your fellow soldiers had fought as well as you did, we would not be talking here."

"Thanks... I suppose."

The silence stretched for a few seconds.

"So, what happens now?" asked Roccafiorita.

"Tomorrow morning, you and your men will be escorted to an area beyond the wire. After that, I don't know. One thing I know, though: for you the war is over."

1. Bardia is a small Libyan town some thirty kilometers west of the Egyptian border where Australian troops fought their first battle of WWII. The battle of Bardia is where the two fictitious characters of Captive Down Under (Rosario Roccafiorita and Giuseppe Pol) were captured. Roccafiorita is imagined to have commanded a post of 75mm Field Guns (63rd Cyrene Division, 45th Artillery Regiment, 2nd Battery) located a few hundred metres south of the "Triangle", a crossing of motor tracks six kilometres south of the town centre. As Craig Stocking reports in his book The Battle of Bardia, Company A of the 7th Battalion, Second Australian Infantry Division, under the

command of Captain J.R. Savige, shortly before 16:00 of January 3rd, managed to capture twelve field guns and take more than 200 prisoners. The book First British offensive in North Africa published by the Italian Army Staff includes a map of the battlefiled that shows the so-called Triangle, which has a side in the North-South direction and a vertex point East. Below the Triangle, the map shows the symbol of a divisional artillery post marked II/45 (2nd battery of Regiment 45).

2. My mother told me that all mail she received from my father when he was serving in Africa had been opened. A web site in Italian shows several examples of censored letters. The letters written by military personnel were censored to protect the confidentiality of troops' locations and movements, but also to isolate the population from information that could feed subversive ideas. The main reason for censoring letters sent to military personnel by their families and friends was to avoid defeatism that could demoralise the combatants. See Appendix E for more info.

3. The Italians expected the British to attack from the south, and concentrated their defences accordingly. The British studied the positioning of Italian units with sorties, overflights, and observation posts. They easily recognised that the Italians were weaker in the north and that they had no mobile quick-response forces to backup the front-line units. Not surprisingly, during the night between the 2nd and the 3rd of January, they attacked from the north.

4. 75 is the caliber of the gun (i.e., the internal diameter of the barrel in mm), while 27 means that the barrel's length is 27 times the caliber. The 75/27 Mod. 1906 were mainly utilised in Northern Africa because of their sturdiness.

   "Saracens" is a medieval term used to identify Muslims. Sicily was a Muslim Emirate from 831 CE to 1072 CE. In this context, "Saracen" refers to a thousand-year-old tree. Note that olive trees can live up to two or three thousand years.

5. The Italian commanders never ordered sorties. This confinement to their posts caused boredom and, perhaps, complacency among the Italian troops. Most importantly, the Italians never had a chance of

discovering that the British were preparing for an attack from the north.

6. A "maestro" is a primary school teacher. A qualification that Mussolini obtained in 1901. Note that in Italy, up to 1997, primary school teachers only needed to complete four years of high school at an Istituto Magistrale, which required one year less than the more prestigious Liceo Classico and Liceo Scientifico and didn't fully qualify the graduate to enter university.

   Roccafiorita's comments place him squarely and unequivocally in the Royalist camp. Roccafiorita's remark about Mussolini's education is somewhat classist, as it is to be expected from somebody with an aristocratic upbringing. But it makes his contempt for the dictator more poignant and immediate.

7. Roccafiorita's questions express my own deep conviction that knowing is accepting, and that an open and multicultural society leads to peace. Indeed, atrocities and crimes against humanity are only possible when "the others" are not seen as fellow human beings.

8. Military training mitigates the fear of battle by creating automatic reactions and stimulating esprit de corps among the troops while driving them to physical exhaustion. Part of military training is indeed to prevent the soldiers from reflecting on what they are supposed to do.

9. According to the GHCN-the daily database maintained by the National Climatic Data Center of NOAA, the minimum temperature in Bardia during the night of January 2nd was between 7°C and 8°C.

10. According to the U.S. Naval Observatory web site, on the night of 2 January 1941, the moon rose over Bardia (31° 46' 0" N / 25° 6' 0" E) at 08:19 and set at 20:09. In any case, being in the fourth day of its cycle, it was only a thin D-shaped sliver. Clearly, the darkness of the night was one of the reasons why the British attacked just then. The moon was going to be full on the 14th, rising at 16:55 and setting at 05:43 of the 15th.

   The name "The Three Merchants" for the costellation of Orion derives from the three perfectly aligned stars that form Orion's belt.

The Pleiades is *my* favourite constellation, perhaps because it was the first one I was able to recognise when I was a Physics student.

11. The description of the battle at Bardia follows what Stockings wrote in *The Battle of Bardia*.

12. In the military, "arty" stands for artillery. An arty spotter, also called artillery or forward observer, is somebody responsible for directing artillery fire onto a designated target.

13. All officers in the Royal Italian Army (RIA) were issued the seven-round semi-automatic Beretta 9mm Model 1934. According to Wikipedia, it remained in service till 1991. The Royal Italian Navy (RIN) was issued a version firing 7.65mm (0.32") rounds. The smaller model (M1935) remained in production till 1967, but my father still had his M1935 when he retired in 1977, a decade later. He had received his first M1935 when he was in the RIN. Then, after the war, when he transferred to the Italian National Police, he managed to hold onto his 7.65 instead of replacing it with the then standard 9mm M1951. He told me that he kept the 7.65 because it was lighter (660g instead of 870g), but I suspect that there was also a sentimental reason! I can testify that it was a very simple weapon to take apart for cleaning and oiling, as I was already able to do it when I was seven years old.

14. Giuseppe "Bepi" Pol appears a few times in *Captive Down Under*. The character is fictitious. Bepi served as a Corporal under Roccafiorita and was captured and sent to Australia with him. Slowly slowly, despite their differences in military rank and cultural background, they developed a friendship. Bepi was a farm hand from the northern region of Veneto, who, before being conscripted, was engaged to a girl he grew up with. Like Roccafiorita, he is an anti-fascist. There was an Amleto Pol among the Italian POWs in Australia who was captured in Libya on 28 March 1941, but he was an AB in the Navy, rather than an Army corporal. I chose the family name Pol because it was the maiden name of my father's mother. Interestingly, Amleto Pol's place of birth was less than 14km away from where my father was born. Many family names from the Veneto region end with a consonant.

15. No need to look for statistics about how tall Italian men were at that time: my father was 175 cm tall, and my mother 164. She told me on

several occasions that in the pre-war Italy their heights were considered to be above average.

More likely, the sergeant was a rugby player, but Roccafiorita would have not considered that possibility because rugby was not a very common sport in Italy.

16. The 2nd Australian Infantry Division was indeed in the battle. And the commanding officer of one of its companies was Captain J.R. Savige, but the name of the sergeant is fictitious. Like in many other occasions, I name a character as a tribute to a real person I know and admire. In this case, McHugh is the name of a well-published Speculative Fiction writer who lives in Canberra, Australia.

Bardia to Maadi – 4-8 January 1941

On the morning of January 4th, Roccafiorita's group, together with dozens of other Infantry and Artillery men, were marched to outside the defence perimeter, where they joined thousands of other prisoners.

As soon as he saw that sea of heads, Roccafiorita knew that the battle for Bardia was lost. The rosary of explosions he could hear in the distance told him that the fighting was continuing, but he felt certain that it was only a matter of time before the last defences would be overwhelmed.

This realisation came with mixed feelings. He was proud of being Italian and the defeat was hard to swallow. He knew that Italian soldiers were capable of selfless acts of heroism. But he also knew that many of the soldiers milling around in the camp with their heads hanging had been drawn into this war against their will. They had been snatched away from their families, dropped into lice-infested rat holes, and told to fight for an alien land of dust, frigid nights, and pitiless sun.

On the 5th, shortly after chaplains had celebrated Mass for the Italian prisoners, the sound of explosions ceased. Perhaps God had listened to the prayers of the many soldiers who had attended. More likely, it was just that the British had finally crashed though the last Italian defences.

The next day, an endless column of trucks moved all the prisoners east, away from future battlefields. Roccafiorita was told to join a group of other young officers on a captured Lancia truck. The highest-ranking among them was a captain of the Blackshirts, who automatically assumed the leading role. (1)

Roccafiorita, after four years of military schools and having attended the Military Academy of Modena, considered the Blackshirts more like misdirected boy scouts than real soldiers. Back at home, they were Mussolini's private militia, often used to impose Fascist rule on civilians, feared by most and hated by many. As military corps, they were poorly trained, better at singing heart-lifting military hymns and scurrilous barracks songs than at fighting.

This officer had probably been promoted to the rank of captain more for his political connections than for his qualities as a leader. The corners of Roccafiorita's mouth edged up into a hint of a smile when he imagined the captain attempting to give orders to the other occupants of the truck. They were all first and second lieutenants, but of the regular army, and he expected that they would simply ignore the captain, despite the three stars on his epaulets and the big eagle on the front of his peaked hat. (2)

For three days they travelled eastward through Egypt along the only available road, which snaked its way close to the Mediterranean coast. Sometimes the briny smell of the sea reached the back of the trucks, and glimpses of its blue waters reached the hearts of the prisoners. They thought of their loved ones who lived beyond those waters, not knowing when they would be able to embrace them again. On the right-hand side, the land was scorched by the baking sun, with some isolated palms and small clusters of sand-coloured houses.

At the end of the second day, they stopped in a small coastal town called El Alamein. The prisoners stretched their backs and flexed their legs to recover from the bumpy ride on the wooden benches of the truck, breathing in the fresh air from the sea and looking at the clear desert sky, full of stars. A hundred metres away, a local man, dressed in the traditional jellabiya, looked on, and Roccafiorita, without really knowing why, waved at him. It was a simple gesture, without any conceivable consequence, but the Blackshirt captain didn't like it. (3)

"What do you think you are doing?" he barked, fists firmly placed on his hips. (4)

"What does it look like?" replied Roccafiorita, who was spoiling for an excuse to knock that arrogant man off his feet.

"You are not supposed to fraternise with the enemy," said the captain, "and I order you to show more respect for your superiors. You will address me as Sir or Captain ..."

"Or else what?" interrupted Roccafiorita. "I don't take orders from you."

The captain's face went through a whole range of reds before he found the words for a reply.

"I will report your insubordination and you will pay for your insolence. You are a disgrace and a shame for all of us."

Roccafiorita was about to jump on the captain when two other officers grabbed his arms and dragged him away.

"Let me go," he kept shouting, "somebody has to teach him a lesson". But the officers, two army lieutenants of about his age, didn't release him until they reached the other side of a parked truck. Roccafiorita was ready to turn his anger from the militia captain to his two restrainers, but when he looked at their faces, he saw that they were smiling. It might have made other people even angrier, but not Roccafiorita. His reaction was to burst into a heart-felt laugh, the anger gone in the blink of an eye. "I gave him a big scare, didn't I?" he said after recovering his breath.

"You could say that," one of the other two replied. "I would have loved to see you smash his nose, but it would have only caused problems. Not worth it.

"Renzi," he added, stretching out his hand. "Giovanni Renzi, and this is my friend Antonio Esposito".

"Rosario Roccafiorita. Thanks for keeping me out of trouble. I should learn to control myself, but I cannot stand arseholes, especially when they wear a uniform."

"Any time!" said Antonio with a wink.

The next morning, Roccafiorita and the Blackshirt captain were directed to board different trucks. Unfortunately, Renzi and Esposito were also transported on another truck.

Shortly after their departure from El Alamein, the road turned south, and they started seeing some cultivated land. After enduring the relentless glare of the sun on rocks and sand, their eyes could finally rest on some green. It was only poor fields at the edge of the desert, but it felt as if they were leaving hell behind and returning to the world of the living.

Before sunset, when the road curved to the left, the men seated close to the back of the trucks saw in the distance the great pyramids of Giza silhouetted against the sky. The prisoners rushed to the back to see them, captivated by the view. For a moment, the war, the dead, and the defeat were forgotten. But only for a moment.

Half an hour later, the two trucks that carried the officers turned off, and departed from the rest of the column. Minutes later, they reached their destination. The prisoners didn't know it, but it was a new facility created only 7 km south of the British General Headquarters specifically for interrogating POWs.

The next morning, Roccafiorita was taken to a small room with two chairs and a small table between them. A clipboard with a note pad and a pencil was resting on the table, and one of the chairs was occupied by a British lieutenant. Roccafiorita sat on the second chair without waiting to be told. The lieutenant's uniform was immaculate. Roccafiorita noticed the folding creases across the front of the officer's khaki shirt, frozen in time by what must have been a very generous dose of starch. The table prevented him from seeing the lieutenant's shoes, but they were undoubtedly spit-polished to a gleaming shine. He suddenly felt somewhat annoyed by the whole setting and couldn't resist the temptation of stretching forward the right leg to place his dirty boot on top of the lieutenant's left foot. There, he thought while suppressing a smile, have a bit of a battlefield on you!

The lieutenant jumped at the unexpected contact, but didn't remark on it. Instead, he leaned forward and grabbed the pencil. "Noumei i iunita?" he asked while holding a pen poised above the notepad.

"Lieutenant Rosario Roccafiorita, 63rd Cyrene Division, 45th Artillery Regiment, 2nd Battery", recited Roccafiorita in English. His English was most likely better than the British officer's Italian, and Roccafiorita saw no reason to submit himself to badly formulated questions in a mangled version of the language he loved.

The lieutenant looked up, his blond eyebrows arched. "You speak English."

Roccafiorita didn't deem the obvious statement to be worth a reply. The lieutenant should have volunteered his name, but Roccafiorita didn't care to know it. He didn't care at all.

"Where did you learn it?" asked the lieutenant.

"In a training camp for Italian spies," said Roccafiorita, barely managing to keep a straight face.

The lieutenant's pale, closely shaved cheeks assumed a colour that would have not been out of place in a fresh-fruit market. But he clearly had been well trained because he managed to hold his temper.

"Place and date of birth?"

"Palermo, 13 December 1918." (5)

"Are you a member of the Fascist party?"

"You should know that you cannot be an officer, commissioned or not, without being a member of the party."

The lieutenant cleared his voice before replying.

"Do you mean to say that you would have not joined if you had not been compelled to do so?"

Roccafiorita understood at once where the lieutenant was going with the interrogation, but saw no reason not to reply honestly and openly.

"My loyalty is to my country and my king," he said.

"You are a Royalist," the lieutenant stated, to which Roccafiorita felt he didn't need to comment.

"Do many of your fellow officers think like you?"

"You'll have to ask them."

"But you don't agree with this war, do you?"

"No. I don't. We fought the Germans when their tribes invaded the Roman Empire, and should have left Hitler to fight his war instead of getting involved. Spain and Portugal didn't join in. We could have done the same. We wouldn't be dying in Greece and Africa if it had not been for the ambition of our Duce." The last word brought a frown to his face. "Duce in Italian means guide, like Führer in German, but what they are leading their nations to is only disaster."

"Would you be prepared to do something about it?"

"Like what?"

"You could do a lot of good for your people and help them free themselves of Mussolini's tyranny. Have you heard of the Free Italy movement?"

Roccafiorita had expected that by professing his antifascism he would open himself to being recruited for political propaganda.

"Look," he said, "I'm not a politician. I am a soldier, and I have taken an oath. I prefer to abide by my oath. Despite my disapproval for the Fascist regime, I will never betray my country. All I can say is that the fortunes of war have been against me and I have nothing further to add". (6)

The next day, it was desert again, eastward, towards Palestine. The Promised Land turned out to be yet another dusty camp in the middle of nowhere, surrounded by barbed wire and a few sentry towers.

"Do lieutenants play cards?"

Roccafiorita was lying on his cot with the hands behind his head. When he opened his eyes, he was rewarded with the sight of a ruddy face covered by a three-day-long red stubble and a lobsided smirk. "Picciotto," he replied without moving, "you must be desperate if you ask me. Are you so short of chickens to pluck?" (7)

The other man, hearing the Sicilian word, broke into a broad smile. "Minchia signor tenente! You are from Sicily!" (8)

Roccafiorita sat on his cot and kept looking at the soldier, who finally realised that the lieutenant was waiting for an answer to his question.

"Well, you have just arrived and I thought you might still have some Italian cigarettes. We get some from the English, but they are not strong enough. They taste like straw." (9)

Roccafiorita jumped off his cot. "I do have half a pack of *Nazionali*. What do we play?"

The smile on the soldier's face broadened. "Do you know *la bestia*?" (10)

"Sure," replied Roccafiorita sitting down together with the red-headed soldier and two of his colleagues.

Less than an hour later, Roccafiorita had before him two packs of Wild Woodbines, a tin marked *Cigarettes*, and a dozen loose cigarettes of various brands. The three soldiers around him looked at his winning pile with a sad face. Roccafiorita, who actually didn't dislike the lighter British cigarettes, split his Nazionali among the soldiers. "So, what has been happening?" He asked after lighting up and plucking a bit of tobacco from the tip of his tongue. (11)

The Sicilian soldier leaned forward and assumed a conspiratorial tone. "I've heard that soon we will be sent to Britain."

The soldier on Roccafiorita's right, a small man with a black mustache that was little more than a thin line above his upper lip, cleared his voice before speaking. "One of the guards told me that we will be sent to India."

The Sicilian laughed. "India? What for?" To which the small one replied with surprising aggressiveness, "And why Britain then? Why not Canada or Australia?"

Roccafiorita knew how it worked: with nothing to do except play cards and football and write letters that might never be delivered, the prisoners spent most of their time speculating about their future and fighting with each other, like roosters cooped up too close together. He withdrew back to his cot leaving on the table half of the cigarettes he had won.

Except for the occasional game of cards, Roccafiorita remained on his own. Some of his fellow prisoners seemed to be OK, and they had all faced the enemy in battle; they had seen death and suffering inflicted on people they knew, and many of them had themselves killed and wounded other human beings. Those shared experiences had left their mark on their spirits and brought them closer to each other, even if nobody talked about what he had seen and done. And yet Roccafiorita preferred to keep his distance. Perhaps it was the precariousness of the situation that forced him to avoid getting attached to anyone. Or perhaps he just needed to heal in silence, like a wounded animal that quietly lies in a corner to licks its cuts and bruises.

But, despite his desire to be on his own, Roccafiorita never missed the opportunity to talk to some of the prisoners who were driven in from the west on an almost daily basis. He didn't know what he was hoping to hear, but he wanted to know what was happening on the front. It was as if he couldn't let go of the war, as if he wanted to be with the soldiers who were fighting and dying only a couple of hundred kilometres away. Unfortunately, the new prisoners invariably brought news of further Italian defeats. In less than a month, first Tobruk and then Benghazi had fallen. Only when the German Afrika Korps arrived, around mid February, the fortunes of war changed: the British and Australian troops, with their supply lines stretched to the maximum, couldn't hold their positions and were forced to retreat. By mid April, the forces of the Axis had pushed the allies all the way through Libya and were knocking at the door of Tobruk

Sergeant McHugh had been right, though: for Roccafiorita the war was over.

1. The Lancia Ro was the most reliable heavy truck of the RIA in WWII. Both the Germans and the Allies were happy to use them.

2. Most Italian officers were considered by the British to be pro-Fascism. Nevertheless, given the traditional rivalry among the Italian armed forces, it is reasonable to assume that many army officers would be reluctant to take orders from a Blackshirt, who belonged to a force considered to be of lower quality and without military tradition.

3. Roccafiorita was captured at the beginning of the Western Desert Campaign, while the Second Battle of El Alamein marks the end of that campaign. But I couldn't resist the temptation to mention it in this story. For many Italians, the battle of El Alamein represents sacrifice and heroism, similarly to what the WWI battle of Gallipoli represents for Australians and New Zealanders. The paratroopers of the 185th Airborne Division Folgore personify that symbol: they managed to hold their positions from 24 October 1942 to 4 November against the 50th, 7th, 44th divisions, and the 1st and 2nd Free French and the Royal Hellenic Brigades. They fought until they ran out of ammunition.

4. This was one of Mussolini's favourite postures, usually with his legs half a meter apart.

5. The date of Decembr 13th, 1918, is of particular significance to me: it was my mother's birth date.

6. I adapted Roccafiorita's reply to the interrogator from a similar statement actually made by Sergeant-Major Lambert Molinelli, a captured Italian pilot, who, according to Moore & Fedorowich, "did not want to seem disrespectful to his interrogators, but freely admitted that he had no intention of giving any information against his country".

Captive Down Under

7. Most Italians with red hair originally come from the regions of Veneto, Sicily, or Tuscany.

   Picciotto is Sicilian dialect for young lad.

   Pollo da spennare (*chicken to pluck*) or, more simply, *pollo* is an Italian expression used to indicate a naive person who can be easily tricked into parting with their money.

8. *Minchia* (in Italiann *ch* is pronounced like *k*) is Sicilian for *cock* (for penis, not rooster), but is much more versatile than its English counterpart. Some men sprinkle it liberally in their language to express surprise or reinforce a statement, like uneducated English people do with four-letter swearwords.

9. Cigarettes have always been a common currency in all detention camps, as those easily available are never enough to satisfy the needs of the heavy smokers.

   The rations of Italian soldiers included cigarettes of the brand Milit, which were strong and without filter. Other brands common in the war years were the *AOI* (Africa Orientale Italiana), *Alfa*, and *Tre stelle* (Three Stars). The *Federazione Italiana Tabaccai* (Italian Federation of Tobacco Merchants) publishes a nice page that shows the historical packaging of cigarettes.

10. *La bestia* (*the beast*) is a quick and heavy gambling game listed in Italy among the games that people are not allowed to play in public places (at least, it was so some time ago). It is a variant of the more gentle *briscola* (*trump*).

11. Wild Woodbines was a brand of cigarettes distributed to the British Army.

Suez to Sydney – 7-25 May 1941

The ship's name was written in huge thick letters on her broadside: Queen Mary. Walking on the pier towards the raft that would take him to the enormous ship, Roccafiorita had mixed feelings. He was happy to leave behind the Middle East, with its dust and its scorpions, but he was again faced with the realisation of how little control he had over his own life. Nobody had bothered to tell the prisoners where they were being taken. "Pack your things" was all they had said, before herding them onto trucks like cattle.

When he reached the deck, a Navy petty officer directed him to his cabin. It was a small cubicle and without a porthole, but at least it was for him alone. There was just enough space for a bed, a cabinet, a tiny table and a chair. *The advantages of being an officer*, he thought.

An area of the main deck was reserved for the prisoners, who were allowed to emerge from their dormitories in groups, following a precise schedule and constantly kept under armed guard. As with the accommodation, Roccafiorita's rank gave him some privileges. After giving his word as an officer that he wouldn't do anything intended to endanger the crew or the ship, he was allowed to spend as much time as he liked in a fenced section of the starboard side of the deck. He was often outside, enjoying the smell of the sea and the occasional shrieking seagull. Especially in the morning, when the ship's superstructure screened the deck from the tropical sun, he liked to sit against the bulkhead and feel through his bones the throbbing of the ship's powerful engines.

Two days after their departure, Roccafiorita saw a low brown coastline almost concealed behind the haze, but still clearly visible, just a few kilometres away. *This must be the Horn of Africa*, he thought. When the next day he saw that the ship was sailing south-east, he knew that they were not sailing around the Cape of Good Hope towards Britain or following the parallel towards India. Their destination was Australia.

I had always wanted to see the land of eucalypts and kangaroos, he reflected. For a fleeting moment, he saw himself strolling along the deck with a beautiful lady on his arm, sipping a glass of chilled champagne. He could almost hear the music spilling out of the glittering ballroom. But on this ocean liner the ballroom was locked up and no champagne was served.

Roccafiorita shared the Officers Quarters aboard the Queen Mary with six other Italian Army officers: one military chaplain and five officers of the medical corps, of whom four were lieutenants and one was a captain. Clearly, their captors intended to look after the souls of their prisoners as well as after their bodies. But why was Roccafiorita on board? It didn't make any sense. He had been trained to lead troops in combat, not to mend their bodies and minds. His initial explanation that his command of English might have been a determining factor became less and less likely when the days passed and nobody called upon his linguistic skills. (1)

To Roccafiorita's dismay, he quickly discovered that his fellow officers appeared to be quite supportive of the Fascist ideology. When the name of Mussolini came up in conversation during the evening meals, the captain's eyes acquired a particular shine, while the chaplain briefly and almost imperceptibly bowed his head, as if the Fascist leader had been a revered saint. The other officers were young men just out of medical school and seemed to have few opinions on their own. Or perhaps they had already learned the prudent strategy of keeping quiet when it came to politics. Although at times Roccafiorita found it difficult to hold his temper, he managed to keep his anti-Fascist ideas for himself and avoid conflict. What was the point? He couldn't possibly hope to convince the captain or the chaplain to abandon their cult of the Duce.

The other officers spent most of their waking hours together with the troops, which left Roccafiorita on his own. Several times a day, he repeated to himself the old proverb *meglio soli che male accompagnati* (better alone than in bad company), but, in reality, he found his isolation like a lead weight on his shoulders.

He exercised on the deck every day, to burn up some energy and help him in his constant battle against boredom. Boredom is the oldest and most relentless enemy of all soldiers and prisoners. With no troops to command and organise and nothing else to do, he had too much time to think about his condition and the family he had left behind in a country at war.

At least his family house was far from military targets. There was no reason for the Allies to drop bombs where his parents, his sister Annunziata, and his brother Salvatore where living.

Salvatore. How he missed him. He wished he could guide him though his teen-age years, protect him from the influence of the regime. At thirteen, Salvatore was still too young to be called to serve in the war. But the regime was relentless in conditioning children into being perfect Fascists. In what other country would a young boy be given a functioning rifle by the state? Roccafiorita balled his fists at the thought of his young brother marching around in black shirt and being indoctrinated with Fascist slogans and songs. (2)

Unfortunately, every day took Roccafiorita farther away from his family, and the dull routine of life on board held him firm in its grip. It started at 6:15 in the morning and ended at ten o'clock in the evening, the only highlights being the four daily meals. Roccafiorita was used to getting up early, but what he couldn't get used to was the oatmeal porridge served at breakfast. He couldn't stand the gluey stuff. There was also always something meaty or fishy, like grilled sausages, bacon, or herrings, but even the thought of eating such greasy stuff first thing in the morning made his stomach contract in disgust. Fortunately, bread with butter and marmalade was also available. Since he was a child, his day had always started with a bowl of old bread covered with a generous amount of sugar and softened with hot milk and coffee. He still remembered entering his family's kitchen, with the bowls of left-over bread around the table and the pervading smell of freshly brewed strong coffee. (3)

At midday, they had their main meal, which consisted of roasted or stewed meat, usually accompanied by soft potatoes and followed by some creamy or mushy sweet. The meat was not bad, but he quickly became saturated by the overcooked vegetables swimming in brown sauce. In the afternoon, they had tea with bread, butter and jam, and another meaty meal in the early evening. The British were clearly doing their best to keep their prisoners well fed.

But everything was so bland! He longed for a plate of pasta in simple tomato and chilli sauce or even a chunk of wholemeal bread with salt and pepper and covered in green olive oil. He also craved red wine to clean the mouth after the fatty meals, a glass of the strong wine that only grapes grown on the black volcanic soil of Sicily can produce.

It was two weeks into their journey, during one of the evening meals, when it happened. They were eating brown beef in a dark brown sauce accompanied by whitish mashed potatoes and pale green peas, but Roccafiorita suddenly saw red. The captain was recounting in lyrical tones how Mussolini had transformed the wetlands around his town into fertile land that produced an abundance of wheat and vegetables. It was nothing special, but Roccafiorita suddenly couldn't take it anymore. (4)

Perhaps it was the boredom of his long days with nothing to do. Or perhaps it was just something bound to happen, driven by an irrepressible force of nature.

He took his plate and threw it across the table, hitting the captain squarely on the face. "Sorry I don't have real shit to serve you with," he said, "but this is pretty close anyway".

For a few seconds, the captain remained as motionless as a statue, with a mix of brown sauce and potato purée trickling down his face to his lap. The other officers looked on in astonishment, their mouths open, the half-chewed meat clearly visible inside them. Then, the captain uttered a roar that had nothing to do with his refined language of a moment before, and launched himself across the table. As the captain slid towards Roccafiorita, plates and glasses scattered in all directions and crashed to the floor as if an earthquake had hit them. Roccafiorita stood up and took a step backward, avoiding the clawing gestures of the captain who, by the time he had come close, was snarling like a rabid dog. It ended as quickly as it had started, when the two lieutenants who had been sitting on either side of Roccafiorita grabbed the captain and held him firm.

The commotion at the officers' table didn't go unnoticed. A wave of silence rolled over the neighbouring tables, as the soldiers turned towards the origin of the fracas, broken a moment later by the frantic whistle of an Australian soldier summoning support. The guards knew they had to react quickly, because small incidents had the tendency to expand into uncontrollable brawls, leading to black eyes and broken bones. A couple of minutes later, all that was left as a reminder of the incident was a table in disarray and a uniform in serious need of cleaning.

It didn't take long for the Australians to figure out that Roccafiorita had been the aggressor, and that his action was totally unprovoked.

"What are you going to do, throw me overboard?" asked Roccafiorita defiantly while standing in front of an Australian Army major. "Or perhaps, as a way of punishment, you will force me to keep sharing my meals with arseholes. Mussolini here, the Duce there... The man deserved what he got."

The major didn't make any effort to suppress a smile. He had an instant liking for this hot-headed officer.

"Lieutenant, I have little patience with Fascists myself. But I cannot tolerate such behaviour. The soldiers don't understand English, and we needed some Italian doctors who could take care of them. And we didn't have much of a choice."

"And why am I here? I don't know how to mend bodies or souls."

"You are here precisely because once we are in Australia we will need somebody to balance the influence of the Fascist officers. From your interrogation in Cairo, it was clear that you were the perfect man for the role. Just tell your people why you don't like Fascism. That's all we ask. Nothing you wouldn't do anyway, would you?" They were also hopeful that the lieutenant would report on the most fanatic Fascists, but the major didn't say it. This Roccafiorita had to be handled like a skittish thoroughbred: firmly but gently.

"So, you're not going to throw me to the fish," Roccafiorita said after a short pause.

The major threw his head back in a burst of laugh. "Certainly not! But from now on, instead of eating with your fellow officers, feel free to pick another table." He looked at Roccafiorita's lapel, where the black, gold-rimmed insignia of his corps was stitched. "We have quite a few artillery men on board. As unlikely as it is, you might even find somebody you know."

Two days later, while having lunch, Roccafiorita was surprised by a familiar voice calling "*Signor Tenente, signor Tenente!*" When he stood up and turned, he found himself face to face with none other than Corporal Pol. They embraced as if they had been brothers, holding back the tears that would have been unbecoming of hardened soldiers.

When they separated, Roccafiorita held his right hand on the corporal's left shoulder. "Isn't it about time that you call me Rosario? After all we have been through and taken together to Australia, we don't need to be so formal. Do we?" Roccafiorita asked with a smile.

Pol's ears acquired a colour between crimson and purple. "I could never do that," he said in a low voice. "You are my superior officer. For me, you will always be *signor tenente*.

"At least," he added with a smile forming on his face, "until you are advanced to captain."

Roccafiorita had to laugh. "OK. As you like. I will remain *signor tenente* and you will remain corporal Pol. But we can still be friends, can't we?"

"It would be an honour," Pol said, his eyes acquiring a shine they didn't have a moment before.

"Yes. It would be, for both of us."

The two men stood quietly before each other, until Roccafiorita broke the silence. "So, my friend, what do you think of our transfer to Australia?"

The answer came back at once, without hesitation. Clearly, Pol had already been reflecting on it. "I think that we are going to be packed away for a long time. They wouldn't send us so far if they thought that we might need to travel back to the Mediterranean any time soon."

"I also think that we should prepare ourselves to a long absence from home. Unless we win the war, that is. But I don't think we will."

Pol arched his eyebrows. After all the brainwashing they had received concerning the glory of Rome and the invincibility of Fascism, Roccafiorita's easy dismissal of a possible victory was not what an officer was supposed to say. (5)

Seeing Pol's surprised expression, Roccafiorita felt he needed to explain himself. "The Germans seem invincible, but they are ruthless aggressors. If there is any justice in this world, the British and their allies will manage to stop them. And Italy, despite what Mussolini might say, is just in the war for the ride, grabbing the tail of their powerful ally and hoping to be able to hang on. In the end, the hubris of Hitler and Mussolini will be their undoing."

Somehow, after Roccafiorita's remarks, it seemed that nothing more could be said. The two men turned towards the railing, rested they elbows on it, and observed the dark water rolling along the side of the ship.

The ship stopped in Fremantle, but there was not much to see, as they were facing away from the pier, towards the broad harbour. A couple of days later, on May 28, 1941, they entered Sydney harbour. (6)

The Queen Mary stopped just before the Harbour Bridge. The prisoners were taken by train through the Sydney suburbs, and there were lots of curious faces lining the backyards of houses facing onto the railway line, staring at them.

1. In reality, only six army officers accompanied the first contingent of 2000 Italian POWs shipped to Australia. Roccafiorita is a completely fictitious character added to those who were actually there.

In the Italian armed forces, all doctors and chaplains are commissioned officers. The doctors are hired after completing their studies and start as full lieutenants. The promotion to the rank of captain comes after only a couple of years of service. This means that the five lieutenants aboard the Queen Mary were very junior, perhaps even drafted into service at the beginning of the war (an unconfirmed possibility).

According to David Cheney's web site, in 2005 there were 32,974 diocesan priests in Italy. With a population of 59,725,000, it means that there was a priest per 1,811 heads of population. Funnily enough, one chaplain for the 2000 POWs in the first shipment of Italian POWs to Australia results in an almost identical ratio. One can only speculate on whether it was the result of a choice or mere coincidence.

Frank Dickinson reports that there were 175,146 physicians in the USA. Wikipedia reports that, according to the 1940 census, the population in USA was 132,164,569. When combined, this two data items result in a physician density of about 1.33‰ (where 1‰ indicates 1 per thousand heads of population). On board the Queen Mary, with five doctors per 2000 prisoners, the physician density was 2.5‰. Very good, although, obviously, it made little difference to the British to send three or five doctors. The WHO reports that in 2010 the physician density in the USA was 2.4.

2. One of the purposes of the *Opera Nazionale Balilla* was to train boys to the use of weapons. Around the age of twelve, the boys were given scaled-dows rifles.

3. The meals described in the paragraph that follows were served on the Hired Military Transport Ship Dunera between 14 and 20 August 1940, as reported by the Hay Historical Society in their book *Haywire*.

4. The reclamation of the Pontine marshes was a major project completed by Mussolini in the early 1930s. It was on 18 December 1932, at the inauguration of the city of Littoria (renamed Latina after the fall of Fascism) that Mussolini said the famous sentence *È l'aratro che traccia il solco, ma è la spada che lo difende* (It is the plow that makes the furrow, but it is the sword that defends it), which captures much of the Fascist ideology in a single slogan. It is interesting to watch how British Pathé reported the event in a video clip titled *Il Duce's Crowning Achievement 1932*.

5. This statement from Roccafiorita should surprise you, considering that in 1941 Germany was winning on all fronts and seemed unstoppable. But I like to make my hero smart!

6. The paragraph that follows is adapted from what Rick Pisaturo wrote on page 35 of his autobiography *Australia, My Love*.

Hay – Thursday 29 May 1941

The train reached Hay at dawn, after a journey of nineteen hours. Roccafiorita was on the first of the four trains that left Sydney full of Italian POWs. Once out of Sydney, it snaked its way through mountainous terrain. The railway line was flanked by trees the prisoners had never seen, and the dense underbrush, at times less than a metre away from the passing train, seemed poised to reassert the supremacy of nature over human engineering. (1)

When the country opened up, the forest gave way to scrubland. Occasionally a farmhouse was visible in the distance, but the countryside that scrolled by outside the train windows showed the prisoners a strange and unfamiliar world. The horizon seemed much farther away than in Italy, and the blue of the sky was more intense. Even more than the three-week journey across the sea, the immensity of the land that had swallowed them made many realise how far they were from home.

At sunset, the temperature fell quickly. With all the windows closed to keep the cold out, the carriages quickly filled up with the acrid smell of sweat mixed with that of dirty socks and of old boots. Roccafiorita was oblivious to the unpleasant smells and the regular bumping of the wheels on the track joints. The moonless night had transformed the world into a sea of pitch-black nothingness, while the sky was resplendent with stars. He stared out of the window, his mind recalling far-away images of his boyhood, when he chased lizards on the stony hills or learned how to open cactus fruits without being pricked by their thorns. (2)

The long journey finally ended and Roccafiorita stepped off the carriage, ready to face whatever the future had in store for him in this alien land.

The prisoners were directed to move westward in a long column which wormed its way at the edge of town. Roccafiorita had to laugh when it occurred to him that the heavy magenta-stained coats they had all received on the pier in Sydney must make the prisoners look like a procession of cardinals. He thought he might start dispensing benedictions to the villagers, but decided for once to exercise some restraint. In any case, they had not far to go, and less than a kilometre from the railway station they turned left into a compound surrounded by three high fences of barbed wire. (3)

A sign hanging outside the exterior gate told the prisoners that they were entering Camp 7. Roccafiorita was directed to the left towards one of the many wooden huts that formed the compound. "Casa dolce casa" ("Home sweet home"), he murmured while pushing the door marked with a stencilled number 1. Inside he saw a dozen two-level bunk beds. As he was the first one in, he chose the top cot closest to the door, climbed onto it, and lay face up, his head resting on his clasped hands, waiting for his room mates to come in. (4)

Being the only officer in his hut, Roccafiorita was designated the hut chief by the camp administration. This made him officially responsible for everyone in Hut 1 to follow the camp rules, which essentially boiled down to showing up on time at morning roll call and keeping the hut in order.

Initially, the other occupants maintained their distance from him, but it didn't take long for them to realise that Roccafiorita, despite his rank, was not enjoying any of the privileges that were usually accorded to Italian officers: he ate the same food, slept in a cot like everybody else, and even shared the same latrines. (5)

Furthermore, when somebody broke some rule, he was ready to shield him from the camp authorities. Instead, he would talk to the offender in private and make him understand that being a prisoner didn't mean that he was no longer a soldier, and that misbehaviour by one man would eventually have consequences for everyone.

From Roccafiorita's point of view, he wasn't doing anything special. He handled the other occupants of Hut 1 more or less as he had handled the men under his command: with respect and compassion, but also making clear that he expected everybody to comply with the rules. The soldiers were not used to officers treating them that way, and quickly began seeing Roccafiorita as a point of reference, as somebody they could ask for advice, usually concerning minor disputes with other prisoners.

But there were also some serious conflicts in the camp. Although the British authorities in the Middle East had intended to avoid sending militant Fascists to Australia, it was inevitable that some would slip through the net. As soon as they arrived in Hay, those fanatics began to establish and enforce a Fascist command structure. (6)

Two of the doctors and the chaplain were at the top of the pro-Mussolini hierarchy, relying on several NCOs and privates to perform acts of intimidation and violence. Although the Fascists steered clear of Roccafiorita, he was kept informed about what was going on by the other prisoners in Hut 1 and by Corporal Pol, whom he met almost every day. (7)

One day, when he walked to meet Pol in Hut 23, Roccafiorita was told that the corporal was in the hospital. A minute later, he was beside the bed where Pol lay with his head bandaged. "What happened to you? Are you OK?" he asked. (8)

"Ah Signor Tenente, I'm all right. They only keep me here to be sure."

"But what happened, dammit?"

"It's nothing. This soldier, Magnani, wanted me to salute him. I said 'Since when do we salute each other? And anyway, I'm the corporal. You should salute me, not the other way round.' He didn't like that and made a sign to somebody behind me I hadn't heard coming. Perhaps he used the handle of a shovel or a peak. Anyhow, he knocked me on the head and here I am. *Questi Fascisti del cavolo sono proprio una rottura di scatole!*" (9)

Just at that moment Captain Del Monte, the senior doctor, entered the hospital hut. A moment later, Roccafiorita was standing before him, his eyes reduced to slits. (10)

"Tell your thugs that they should leave my men in peace," he said with so much venom in his voice that the captain took a step back.

"Your men? You mean the sissies who bend over to please our enemies? We have no patience with collaborators."

Perhaps the captain had allowed himself to provoke Roccafiorita because he felt safe in his medical world, where he was the boss, with a stethoscope in the pocket of the white coat and with orderlies ready to jump at his beckoning. He could have not been more mistaken. Roccafiorita's hands were already balled into tight fists. All he needed to do was bring one of them to shoulder height and project it forward. The captain's reflexes turned out to be quite good, and he almost managed to avoid the punch. His luck, because otherwise his jaw would have certainly shattered. But he still found himself seated on the floor without knowing how he got there, his ears buzzing as strongly as a swarm of angry bees.

Roccafiorita licked the knuckles of his right hand with a grimace, waved the other hand to Pol, and walked around the captain to exit the hospital. There was nothing more to be said. He had made himself clear enough. Hadn't he?

He expected that the captain would report him to the camp authorities and was not disappointed: before the day was over, he was summoned to the office of Lieutenant Colonel Thane, the camp commander.

"Lieutenant, you know I cannot let you get away with it, don't you?"

"Yes Sir. I know."

"What did you think you were doing?"

"Punching an arsehole, Sir, if I may use the expression."

The colonel laughed.

"Is that your standard strategy? First do what you want and then ask for permission?"

Roccafiorita understood perfectly well that the colonel was referring to the expletive, but couldn't miss the opportunity to play with it.

"Why, Sir, would you have allowed me to punch Captain Del Monte if I had asked you in advance?" His face remained perfectly serious.

Another burst of laughing. "I like you Roccafiorita. You make me laugh. But you should control your temper. Sooner or later, it will get you into serious trouble. Anyhow, violence cannot be tolerated and I cannot risk that it gets out of hand."

"I understand, Sir, but what about the Fascists? Why do they get away with their beatings?"

The colonel reflected for a moment before replying. "They are smart enough to do it when no guard is around. That's why. And those who are beaten up seldom report the incidents."

Roccafiorita moved his weight from one foot to the other. "So, what now, Sir?"

"Now you will enjoy three weeks of isolation in a punishment cell." (11)

"It will have been worth it. Every day of it!" replied Roccafiorita with a bright smile.

The colonel shook his head and summoned the guard.

1. The figure of nineteen hours for the trip from Sydney to Hay comes from the web site "Hay Internment and POW Camps Interpretive Centre". I use it in preference to the "two or three days" reported by Rick Pisaturo on page 35 of his autobiography, mainly because Pisaturo doesn't provide a precise duration. Perhaps those 19 hours seemed to Pisaturo much longer than they actually were!

2. The centre of our galaxy, the Milky Way, is only visible in the southern hemisphere. As a result, the southern sky has more visible stars and, in particular, more first-magnitude stars.

3. Luigi Bortolotti was one of the 2000 Italian POWs who arrived in Australia in May 1941. In his diary, as reported by O'Connor, he wrote *Ci distribuiscono [...] un pastrano rosso. Sembriamo tutti cardinali (We are issued with a red overcoat. We all look like cardinals).*

   Inside the front cover of *Haywire* is a map with the location of the camps. By matching the names of the streets shown on that map with those shown on the corresponding Google map, I managed to estimate a distance of between 900m and 1000m.

4. I was unable to establish the presence of the stencilled hut number as an historical fact, but the military tradition in all countries that I know of is to post signs everywhere and mark everything. It would be inconceivable for a military compound not to have a sign outside the main entrance or to have unmarked buildings. There were three camps in Hay, numbered 6, 7, and 8, each with a capacity of 1000 prisoners. The Italians were kept in 7 and 8, which were close to each other on the western side of the town. On the east of town, camp 6 was built after the other two and held Japanese.

The number of beds is an approximate estimate based on the fact that each camp held 1000 prisoners and on the map shown in appendix F, 36 huts can be counted: 1000/36 = 28 prisoners per hut, corresponding approximately to a dozen bunk beds. The estimate is also based on drawings made by Emil Wittenberg, one of the German internees who occupied camp 7 before the Italian POWs (Haywire, pp 30 and 31).

5. Italian officers were known for living in what could only be called luxury even when stationed very close to the front. When the Australian and British soldiers conquered command posts (e.g., in Bardia and Tobruk) previously occupied by Italians, they found white linen and fine wines.

6. Moore & Fedorowich report that "the efforts by the Fascists to maintain their party structure [within the camp] posed an immediate challenge to the POW authorities at Myrtleford" and that a "young lieutenant had been removed from his post as medical officer at Hay because of his Fascist activities".

7. Actually, the priest who was a recognised Fascist was Padre Faustino Lenti in Cowra. Still according to Moore & Fedorowich, a junior medical officer was transferred before 1944 from Hay to Myrtelford for his Fascist militancy. Lt. Donati, one of the five doctors included in the first shipment of Italian POWs, was indeed transferred from Hay to Myrtleford on 31 March 1942 via Murchison (1 April 1942 to 10 June 1942), but there might be other officers that would fit the bill. I have no information concerning the political orientations of the five doctors and the chaplain who arrived in Australia in May 1941.

8. I have not been able to find a precise reference with the physical size of the camp, but if you look at the second of the two maps I included in the description of Camp 7 in appendix F, you will see that the hospital (marked "C1" and "C2") is not farther away from Hut 23 than the length of a football field.

9. According to Moore & Fedorowich, the Fascists claimed that the hierarchy they established in the camps overrode the military one.

Questi Fascisti del cavolo sono proprio una rottura di scatole means *These bloody Fascists are really breaking my balls*. The expression *del cavolo* (literally, *of the cabbage*) actually refers to the penis and *scatole* (literally, *boxes*) refers to testicles. The terms *cavolo* and *scatole* are euphemisms for *cazzo* (i.e., cock in the sense of penis) and *palle* (i.e., *balls*). Such euphemistic terms were often used in the 1900s to make the sentence less vulgar, and are nowadays out of fashion.

10. The name *Del Monte* (which means *Of the Mountain*) is a fictitious name. The actual name of the captain of the Army Medical Corps in Hay was *Della Valle* (which means *Of the Valley*). I changed the name to prevent any casual reader from assuming that Captain Della Valle was a Fascist activist. I have no reason to believe that he actually was. An irrelevant but nice piece of trivia: Della Valle had his 45th birthday eight days after arriving in Hay.

11. Moore & Fedorowich report: "According to Dr. G. Morel, the Swiss representative of the ICRC who made his first POW inspection at Hay in August 1941 [,...] A total of 42 punishments had been meted out [... ranging] from one day to 28 days". Quite a few, considering that the camp had only been established in June 1941.

Hay & Cook – 1941/1942

When Roccafiorita emerged from his cell, he noticed that several of his fellow inmates wandered about like sleep-walkers. Within the short period of a few weeks, the dull routine of life in captivity was already taking its toll. *How will these people cope in the months and years to come?* he asked himself with sorrow. He went at once to the camp's office and asked to talk with the commander.

Col. Thane was a busy man, but Roccafiorita's unexpected request made him curious. The following afternoon, the Italian lieutenant was once more standing before the commander's desk.

"Congratulations lieutenant! You have been out of isolation for longer than twenty-four hours and nobody has yet filed a complaint against you! Hope your health is OK."

Roccafiorita replied with a grin. "I'm fine, Sir. Thanks for asking." He wasn't a man to beat about the bush, and went straight to the point. "I asked to talk with you because I'm concerned about my fellow prisoners."

The intent look on the colonel's face encouraged Roccafiorita to continue. "They are bored to death, Sir. Football and playing cards are not enough to keep them busy, and there is only so much that they can write to their families when the most exciting event in days is a clogged latrine. I'm also concerned that the Fascists will find fertile ground for their propaganda. They don't miss an opportunity to foment dissent, and it will not take long before you will have to deal with serious problems and even sabotage." (1)

The colonel nodded. "I know. And my superiors know it too. Soon there will be a library and I'm trying to find some films in Italian, but everything takes time."

"Sir, find them work to do. Many of them are labourers, and used to working hard. We have carpenters and artisans. Let them convert a hut to a workshop and give them some tools. Perhaps you could also let them build a church." (2)

Unbeknown to Roccafiorita, the Australian government was keen to put the prisoners to work, but the wheels of bureaucracy were grinding slower than all parties involved would have liked. (3)

For thirty long seconds, the colonel sat like a statue, his eyes pinned on Roccafiorita's but without seeing. Then, he blinked. "OK lieutenant, you'll get your tools. But I will hold you responsible for your workers. If they use the tools to dig a tunnel or cut the fence and escape, I promise you that you will only see the sun through bars for a long time. Try to involve as many prisoners as possible. Rotate them if necessary. And include some moderate Fascists". Thane was not looking forward to informing his superiors of what he was doing, but the young Italian officer was right. The colonel also knew that if he had asked for permission in advance instead of relying on a fait accompli, they would have never agreed. (4)

Leaving the commander's office, Roccafiorita couldn't help thinking that, had he been an Australian lieutenant in an Italian POW camp, he would have not even been able to talk with the camp commander. Officers of Mussolini's militia didn't waste time with prisoners. (5)

The next months passed for Roccafiorita in a blur. He started by picking a group of two sergeants and four corporals who had experience in construction. (6)

Their task was to build a hut that could be used as a church. For experienced carpenters and construction workers, the job was not difficult. The main problem was that almost everybody in the camp wanted to contribute. It took longer than a week just to agree on who would do what. Roccafiorita could have cut short the endless discussions, exercised his authority, and settled any dispute "by diktat". After all, they still were in the military. But that would have defeated his purpose. He wanted to get the men involved, and animated discussions were a sign of involvement. He intervened only on the occasions when he realised that the arguments were caused by clashing of egos rather than resulting from genuine issues.

On Advent Sunday the church was finally inaugurated. Most of the worshippers had to stand outside, and the high temperature, well above the thirty-degree mark, combined with the ever-present dust and the relentless sun, made the experience a test of endurance. (7)

Christmas was rapidly approaching, but the prisoners couldn't get into the right spirit to celebrate it. It didn't feel right to think of a donkey and an ox warming up baby Jesus with their breath when the sun burned like hell and the heat was intense. The candles that the camp administration had provided for the church succumbed to the heat and bent like wilting flowers. A resourceful soldier had the idea of tying them up to thin sticks to keep them straight, but they still didn't feel right.

Despite the heat, Christmas came to pass and, by the beginning of 1942, most prisoners had settled in and found ways to keep themselves busy. Col. Thane had managed to find several dozen books in Italian, which were constantly in circulation, even if some of them were children's book like "Le avventure di Pinocchio" and "Il giornalino di Gianburrasca"; but the most popular books were the action adventure novels that Emilio Salgari had written for young adults. (8)

Besides the mainstay of regular football matches that quickly developed into well attended tournaments, manicured small orchards also distracted the prisoners' minds from their condition of captivity, and some of them also tried their artistic skills at carving, drawing, or painting.

Political strife never entirely disappeared, but the opposing factions of Fascists and anti-Fascists managed a pragmatic truce that only occasionally exploded into open conflicts and fist-fights. It was perhaps this détente more than anything else that affected Roccafiorita's mood, as the newly-found, albeit precarious, peace robbed him of an outlet for his frustration at being in captivity. Moreover, organising the establishment of a workshop and the construction of the church had only been possible by reaffirming his authority as an officer, which in turn kept him isolated from the other prisoners. Even Pol, to whom he felt very close, still insisted on calling him "Signor Tenente". And he certainly had nothing to say to the other few officers present in the camp. As far as he was concerned, they were just good at polishing the golden stars on their epaulettes.

"Run out of things to do, have you?"

"Couldn't put it better myself, Sir," Roccafiorita replied while standing once more in Colonel Thane's small office.

Thane had seen other young officers like Roccafiorita. The best of them were the same, regardless of their creed or colour: flaring their nostrils and pawing until they were let out to run across the fields. Pity you are not one of ours, he thought. *I would send you at once to fight the Germans. But, perhaps, I can let you out of this cage, at least for a while.* (9)

"You want to get out of here."

"Guilty as charged... Sir."

"I have been asked to provide prisoners to work on the Trans-Australia railway line. It will be hard work, but it's the only thing I can offer. As an officer, you cannot be forced to do physical work, but you can volunteer for it."

Roccafiorita replied without hesitation, a smile slowly illuminating his face. "I do. I volunteer."

"OK then. I will have to transfer you to Loveday in South Australia and from there you will be detached to Labour Camp No. 3 in Cook. (10)

"Sir, is there any chance that I could be listed as a non-commissioned officer?"

When Thane looked up with his eyebrows raised, Roccafiorita felt he needed to explain himself. "You know, as an officer, I will always be treated like a strange animal, as if I were a spotted zebra or a black swan". (11)

Thane exploded in a sonorous laugh. It took him several seconds before he could reply to Roccafiorita. "Sorry, Lieutenant. I'm not laughing about you. It's just that... You see, ... In Australia we don't have zebras, but all our swans, believe it or not, are black!

"I know what you mean", the colonel continued while still dabbing his eyes with a handkerchief, "but I cannot alter your papers. You'll have to deal with the issue yourself."

Several days later, after a journey of 1,700 km mostly across desolate landscapes, Roccafiorita stepped off a truck at the edge of a tent camp. When the driver stopped the engine, the only sounds Roccafiorita heard were the dogged buzzing of flies and the whistling of wind. He was a Sicilian and had endured the heat of the Libyan coastal desert and the dryness of Hay better than many others, but the environment he now found himself in set new standards for what the words sun, heat, and dust could possibly mean.

The driver hopped off down from the truck's cabin, cheerfully exclaimed: "Welcome to Cook, mate!", and walked towards the camp without saying a word. Roccafiorita shouldered his sack and hurried behind him.

Cook was very different from Hay. For one thing, there were no barbed-wire fences and no guard towers. The guards were very few and often unarmed. Apart from the fact that the trucks were locked and kept under 24-hour surveillance, it could have been a boy-scout camp. Miles and miles of harsh terrain in all directions were enough to discourage even the most daring of potential escapees. The township was dozens of miles away and, even if an escapee had managed to survive the long march through the desert and avoid being bitten by scorpions and some of the deadliest venomous snakes on Earth, he would have found himself among a small bunch of houses where he would stick out like a sore thumb.

Roccafiorita was happy to find out that most of the prisoners were internees, rather than POWs. They were Italians or naturalised Australians of Italian origin who had been in Australia when Italy entered the war. The Australian authorities had interned them as 'enemy aliens' for reasons of national security. The presence of only a few POWs freed Roccafiorita from the concern that he would find himself isolated, as he had been in Hay. The internees were civilians, not intimidated by the fact that he was an officer. Roccafiorita had already prepared himself to tell other POWs that he was in fact a sergeant who had disguised himself as an officer to receive better treatment from his captors. But lying was against his grain, and not having to invent a fake identity was much preferable to the alternative. (12)

In principle, the job of the prisoners was simple: replace worn or cracked railway sleepers and ensure that the railroad bed and the rail joints were firm and stable. In practice though, the relentless sun, heat, dust, and flies meant that the workers had to make frequent stops to drink water and rest a bit in the shade. As a result, work proceeded much more slowly than it would have in a temperate and shady place. Despite the harsh conditions though, Roccafiorita quickly discovered that he liked the work in that pitiless environment. At least, he was doing something useful. The climate was more extreme than in central Sicily, but not very different from it. And, although he saw no reason for attempting an escape, which in any case would have been almost suicidal, he liked that he was no longer surrounded by barbed wire.

Both the prisoners and the guards were lodged in large tents. Every couple of weeks, as work along the railway line proceeded, the prisoners took the tents apart and loaded them onto trucks, so that the whole camp could be moved further West. (13)

Initally, the internees with whom Roccafiorita shared the tent were somewhat diffident towards him. Perhaps they held him in part responsible for their predicament. After all, he was an officer in the Italian army, and they would have not been taken from their homes if people like him had not fought on the side of Germany. But they quickly realised that he was against the war as much as they were, and much farther away from his family than they were from theirs. It took only a few days for the other occupants of his tent to accept him as one of them.

For Roccafiorita and the other prisoners and internees, life became a series of routines that spanned the whole day, from the moment they were woken up to when they went back to their tents for the night. The heat and the hard work under the punishing sun left little energy for anything else. Before sleeping, some wrote to their families and others played *briscola* or *scopa*. The climate and the repetiveness of the work had the combined effect of dulling the senses, placing everyone, captives and guards, into a state of semi-permanent sleepiness that even swarms of flies didn't manage to break. When the order to transfer him back east came through, Roccafiorita was surprised to realise that already longer than a year had gone by on the railway. (14)

1. The map of the camp drawn by one of the prisoner (see appendix F) shows a football field.

2. If you look at the two maps of Camp 7 shown in appendix F, you will notice that the map drawn by a prisoner includes a workshop and a church that are missing in the official map.

3. Moore & Fedorowich, quoting from original sources, report: "Most telling was the [Australian Military] Board's conclusion 'that the national benefits to be derived from the acceptance by the

Captive Down Under

Commonwealth Government of these prisoners of war are considerable'".

4. These events are fictitious. The only historical fact is the presence of a workshop and of a church, but I don't know when they were built. Several sources, including *Haywire*, report that the POWs were used for construction work within the camp.

5. This is pure speculation on my part, only aimed at expressing from a new angle Roccafiorita's anti-Fascism. But it is a reasonable assumption, as the Blackshirts' cultivated an image of toughness and were the Italian equivalent of the German SS, who were in charge of the concentration camps.

6. Rank and profession of all POWs are available for viewing and download on the web site of the NAA. Although I haven't examined in detail the records of the first 2000 POWs, an examination of 638 of the more than 18,400 records showed that 107 POWs had suitable professions. Also, 118 POWs were corporals or sergeants. It can therefore be estimated that perhaps 60 men had suitable ranks and professions (107/638 x 118/638 x 2000).

7. Advent Sunday is the fourth Sunday before Christmas Day. In 1941, it was November 30. Note that I don't actually know when the church was inaugurated. That is, I set the date arbitrarily, without any historical foundation.

   The daily global historical climatology data provided by the National Climatic Data Center of the NOAA doesn't include temperature data for Hay. But, during the last five days of November 1941, the maximum temperatures in Canberra were 30.8, 31.4, 24.4, 33.7, and 33.8 degrees centigrade, and Hay tends to be at least a couple of degrees warmer than Canberra.

   NOAA reports that, from June to November 1941, Hay only received an average of 18.3 mm of rain (20.3, 20.8, 18.3, 17.4, 20.1, 12.7).

8. Written by Carlo Lorenzini under the pen name of Carlo Collodi, "The Adventures of Pinocchio" tells the story of an animated marionette on its journey to become a real boy. It was first published in 1883. Pinocchio's nose grew after every lie, and his quest to become human

became a symbol for emancipation. Even two episodes of "Star Trek - The Next Generation" mentioned Pinocchio when referring to the character Lieutenant Commander Data, who was an android (i.e., a humanoid robot). Pinocchio was first mentioned in "Encounter at Farpoint", when Data first appears, and the second time in "The Measure of a Man" (my favourite episode of TNG) when Commander Riker proclaims "Pinocchio is broken; its strings have been cut" after switching Data off.

I could't find any English translation of *The giornalino di Gian Burrasca*, which was written by Luigi Bertelli under the pen name Vamba and first published in 1912. It is surprising that this delightful novel was never translated, as everybody I know in Italy read it as a child. "Giornalino", in this context, stands for "journal" or "diary". "Gian" stands for "Gianni", which translates to Johnny, and "burrasca" means "storm". "Gianburrasca" is therefore a nickname that gives an idea of the tempestuous behaviour of the main character.

Every 20th-century Italian teenager (at least up to the baby boomers, including me) must have read several of the eighty novels written by Salgari. That the POWs read fiction written for children and youth is speculation on my part, but many of the prisoners were labourers with minimal schooling. It is therefore reasonable to assume that they would enjoy reading gripping stories written in simple language.

9. It is mid March 1942. In North Africa, Rommel is pressing from the West against the Gazala line of defence of the allied forces, forty miles west of Tobruk. Rommel broke through at the end of May.

10. The Loveday Prisoners of War Group officially opened near Barmera in June 1942, but by then two Internment Camps had been operating in the same location for one year (AWM).

The NAA's web site states that "300 Italian internees were employed as railway workers at Cook on the Trans–Australia line", while Wikipedia includes the Cook's labour detachment in its list of WWII's POW camps in Australia. The fact that Cook also held POWs is confirmed by the Service and Casualty Form of the Italian POW Mario Bonato (PWI 45055), which reports that Bonato was sent to the Labour Detachment No. 3 in Cook from 15 April 1942 to 31 August 1943. Furthermore, the

Reports on the Directorate of Prisoners of War and Internees at Army Headquarters, in disagreement with what reported on the AWM web site, states that "300 Italian PW [were employed at Cook, South Australia] on re-sleepering and maintenance work on the East-West railway."

11. In Italian, like in English, the odd member of a group is said to be a black sheep. But in Italy, all swans are white, and it seemed nice to play on the fact that in Australia the native swans are all black.

12. As at December 1942, 3,836 Italians were held in Australian internment camps (AWM). Approximately 300 of them were in Cook.

13. The fact that the camp moved as the railway line was built is another one of my speculations, but it was a standard practice whenever long overland lines were built around the world, so as to minimise the usage of fuel needed to ferry the prisoners between their accommodations and the construction sites.

14. *Briscola* and *Scopa* are traditional Italian card games played with 40 cards (1 to 7 plus Jack, Queen, and King).

When I was a boy, I bought a plastic fly and put it in the middle of my father's plate. His only reaction was to push the fly to the edge of the plate before beginning to eat. When I expressed my disappointment at his lack of reaction with tears and loud protests, he said something like: "A fly is nothing. In Ethiopia, during the war, if I had not eaten because of flies in my plate, I would have starved."

Cowra – Tuesday 27 July 1943

Lulled by the rocking of the carriage over the uneven tracks, Roccafiorita looked at the fields gliding by, his eyelids drooping. He was suspended in a world between wakefulness and dreams where time had no meaning. Outside his metal cradle, he saw a land that the cold light of the full moon had robbed of all reality. When he finally slid into sleep, the alien land morphed into the familiar hills of his native Sicily, and a moment later he was leading his men into battle surrounded by the dunes of the African desert. Images of peace and war chased each other like wooden horses on a merry-go-round, faster and faster but without going anywhere. (1)

The next day began with the screech of brake blocks against metal. The train was entering a station. Roccafiorita didn't manage to read its name, but he didn't really care. Those names with too many consonants and double Os didn't mean anything to him. Somebody will certainly tell me when I will have arrived, he thought.

Laying railway tracks under the scorching South Australian sun would have taken a toll on most men, but the last sixteen months had been good for Roccafiorita. His skin was burned, his hands calloused, and his finger nails broken like those of all other prisoners who had been assigned to Cook, but the monotonous hard labour had had on him the effect that others could have found in meditation: for the first time in his life, he felt calm and in peace with himself. He hadn't lost the impatience and hot headedness that so many times had gotten him into trouble, but now he was able to control them. At least, so he felt.

Roccafiorita's destination was the POW Camp No. 12, three kilometres north east of Cowra, in New South Wales. *Back in the cage*, he thought while crossing the triple barbed-wire fence through the main gates. (2)

He was sent to camp C, one of the two sections of the compound where the Italians were held. As soon as he entered the camp from the main thoroughfare of the compound he was surrounded by complete chaos. The prisoners, gathered in small groups throughout the camp's grounds, were engaged in animated discussions, their arm flailing the air. Emotions were clearly running high, and several guards moved slowly through the clamouring crowd while holding their batons ready to break up any fist fight that might get started. (3)

Looking for hut number seven, to which he had been assigned, Roccafiorita walked by a group of four prisoners who were speaking in Sicilian dialect. Three of them were arguing loudly, while the fourth one seemed content to listen, with a faint smile on his lips.

"What's going on?" Roccafiorita asked in dialect, dropping his sack beside the quiet one.

The man, an infantry sergeant, turned towards Roccafiorita raising his right hand with all five fingers brought together. "What do you mean, what's going on?" he said. (4)

"What is everybody arguing about?" asked Roccafiorita. "I have just arrived from a camp in South Australia and would like to know what all this discussing is about."

The man burst into laughter before shouting towards the other three "Picciotti, u tenente nunn'u sa'!" ("Boys, the lieutenant doesn't know it!"). He then turned again towards Roccafiorita and told him: "Mussolini is gone! The king has dismissed him! Fascism is dead!". (5)

The four men looked at Roccafiorita waiting for his reaction with an expectant expression on their faces, but the news had left the lieutenant speechless. When he recovered from his surprise, several seconds later, Roccafiorita slapped the sergeant on the back and said what probably was on everybody's mind: "Without Mussolini, we will stop fighting the English, won't we? Soon the war will be over and we'll be going home!". He couldn't suppress a tremor in his voice and barely managed to prevent the wetness in his eyes from spilling over.

"Right," said the sergeant. "That is precisely what we were discussing about. It was Mussolini that brought us into this war to show off with his buddy Hitler. With Mussolini gone, how long before we stop fighting the allies? The king surely will want to make peace." (6)

Roccafiorita nodded in agreement. Two weeks earlier, he had been shocked by the news that the British and their American allies had landed on Sicily and worried that his family could be caught in the crossfire. But the news of Mussolini's fall was truly astonishing. Will the King and

Badoglio seek peace with the British? And if that happened, what would the Germans do? (7)

The life in the camp returned to an apparent normality, but it felt like the calm before a storm. The atmosphere was electric, full of expectation, as if the Italian POWs were collectively holding their breaths. Roccafiorita received his identity card and settled down in hut number seven, but found it extremely demanding to subject himself to the routine of the camp. (8)

And then it happened. On the 9th of September, the announcement came that Italy had ceased all hostilities against the Allies. For Italy, the war was over, or so everybody thought. If the announcement of Mussolini's fall had sparked among the prisoners heated discussions, the end of the war was welcomed by everyone. (9)

But the momentous event, despite its historical significance, was a letdown for the prisoners, as it had absolutely no impact on camp life: the armed guards kept watching the compound from high observation towers; the routines remained unchanged; and, most importantly, the barbed wire stayed up. Delegations of prisoners went to the camp commandant and asked to be freed, as Italy was no longer at war with Australia, but the requests didn't achieve any result. (10)

Different office, different camp, but Roccafiorita was once more standing two paces away from the commandant's desk. The commandant of Cowra's camp C, Major Timms, was a peaceful-looking man in his late forties with a round face and an incipient baldness. The major appraised Roccafiorita through his wire-rimmed spectacles and immediately saw that the soldier standing before him was a man of character. The expression on Roccafiorita's face was one of defiance, with his jaw firmly clenched, his chin projected forward, and his intelligent gaze unflinching. (11)

"I'm told that you speak fluent English," said Timms to break the ice.

"Yes Sir." And, after an almost imperceptible pause, "Sir, I want to go back to Italy and fight the Germans."

The major laughed. "You don't beat about the bush, do you?" he said.

"No Sir. I don't. Now that Mussolini is gone and Italy is fighting against Hitler's troops, I want to do my part and drive the Germans out of my country. I have spent almost three years behind barbed wire or building a railway line. It is time that I resume my job as a soldier. You will understand that."

The major stood up, walked around his desk, and stopped before Roccafiorita, his eyes pinned on the lieutenant's. "I do, lieutenant, I really do. The Japanese are as ruthless and fanatic as the Nazis, and they are knocking on our door. I am a patriot as you are, and, like you, would like to fight our enemies on the front to defend my country. But, as you are an officer, you will know that not everyone can fight a war by charging enemy lines with a bayonet at a ready. Some of us must remain behind and support our fighting troops from home." (12)

"With all due respect, Sir," said Roccafiorita between clenched teeth, "I am a professional soldier, not a farmer or a carpenter that Mussolini forced into a uniform to satisfy his delusions of grandeur. My place is at the front, fighting for the freedom of my country. What good can I do locked up in a dusty camp at the other end of the world?"

Major Timms walked back behind his desk before replying, with an expression on his face that added at least five years to his age. "You are right. You should go back and fight the Germans. And I assure you that if I had any way to help you do that, I wouldn't hesitate for a single moment. But I have my orders, and they don't involve shipping you back to Italy. I'm sorry."

Clearly, there was nothing more to be discussed, and Roccafiorita left the commandant's office without saying a word and without closing the door behind him.

After his encounter with the commandant, Roccafiorita entered a phase of despondency. He had always found it difficult to be behind barbed wire, but his imprisonment suddenly became almost intolerable. Frustration and a feeling of powerlessness fuelled inside him a rage that made his temper even more volatile than usual. He got involved in more and more arguments that not always remained verbal, and other prisoners learned that it was prudent to give him a wide berth when their paths crossed with his. For a man of action like Roccafiorita, there was only one way to move forward: escape.

Roccafiorita quickly discarded the idea of digging a tunnel under the double fence that surrounded the camp. It was too much work for one man and he didn't feel like involving other prisoners in his escape. He also excluded the possibility of overpowering a guard and using him as a hostage. He didn't like the idea of resorting to violence against the guards and, in any case, he felt that it wouldn't succeed.

The simplest solution was to be assigned to one of the parties that exited the camp to work, pick up material, or dispose of garbage. Once outside, he was confident that he would be able to sneak away. After Italy had signed a peace treaty with the allies, the attitude of the guards towards the Italian POWs had somewhat relaxed. And the scarlet dye of their prisoner's clothing had faded away. Not completely, but enough to make them less conspiquous. His good command of English would also serve him well in allaying suspicion when talking with people outside the camp.

Having made up his mind, he felt better. All he needed to do was manage to be assigned to a task outside the camp. Or, perhaps, he could find somebody with an outside assignment who would agree to swap places. It would probably cost him a week of cigarette allowance, but it would be worth it.

What would he do once at large? Where would he go? He had no idea, but it didn't really matter. His mind was made up. He spent the next couple of weeks studying the schedules of activities, familiarising himself with the guard assignments, and finding the most faded pieces of clothing. With Christmas rapidly approaching, there seemed to be more tasks involving crossing the wire. It would have to be soon. Very soon.

But his plans to escape were thwarted whe on the next day, less than a week before Christmas, Roccafiorita was transferred out of Cowra. Like most other Italian POWs, he was sent to work on a farm.

The train travelled North, and then East, and then North again, with two connections at stations that were in the middle of nowhere. He left Cowra in the early morning together with a dozen other prisoners, and only arrived at his destination, the small town of Glen Innes in New South

Wales, after sunset. They were marched through a fence that enclosed what looked like military barracks. After being fed a thick soup that might have once even contained some meat, the prisoners were directed to a big tent, where they spent the night. (13)

In the morning, a truck took Roccafiorita and the other prisoners to their new homes.

1. Actually, the full moon was on July 17th, and by the 26th, when Roccafiorita was travelling towards Cowra, it was already less than half full. But I took a "poetic licence" because I liked the image of the full moon illuminating the barren landscape. In a few paragraphs, it will become clear why I wanted my protagonist to travel on the 26th rather than on the 17th, when the moon was actually full.

2. The distance of the camp from Cowra, according to the document "Cowra Prisoner of War Campsite", was two miles. You can see the location of the camp on Google Maps.

   Cowra was one of the three largest POW camps in Australia, the other two being Murchison in Victoria and Loveday in South Australia, each designed to hold up to 4000 prisoners (AWM).

   Australian POW camps were surrounded by two or three barbed-wire fences varying in height from six to ten feet (AWM).

3. The main thoroughfare through the camp was named Broadway, perhaps simply because it was indeed quite wide.

4. The gesture with the fingers joined accompanied by a small movement forth and back of the forearm without bending the wrist, means "What?". It is known throughout Italy, but mostly used in the southern regions. I found it disconcerting and somewhat rude when I asked a passer-by for street directions in Tel Aviv and he replied to me with that gesture. It turned out that in Israel that exact same gesture means "Wait a minute!"

5. *Picciotti, u tenente nunn'u sa'* is a phrase in Sicilian dialect that in Italian would be: "*Ragazzi, il tenente non lo sà!*".

Australian newspapers of 27 July 1943 reported these events on their front pages. See for example "The Canberra Times", Vol. 17, No. 4792.

6. The sergeant is not exacly right: Mussolini entered the war because he expected the Germans to win it soon and, by joining in, he thought Italy could share in the victory with a limited investment (similarly to what Italy did in WWI). Many sources agree on that. For example, the Italian journalist and historian Indro Montanelli, possibly one of the greates Italian journalists of the 20th century, in his *Storia d'Italia* (*History of Italy*), states that "*[Mussolini] in guerra si decise ad entrare solo quando credette che fosse già vinta*" (*[Mussolini] decided to enter the war only when he believed that it had already been won*).

Italy signed a peace treaty with the allies about one and a half months after the fall of Fascism, from 25 July to 8 September 1943.

After the fall of Fascism, it was easy to exonerate the king of Italy of responsibilities, while in fact he had acquiesced to Mussolini's dictatorship for two decades. On 2 June 1946, enough Italians disagreed with the forgiving opinion expressed by the sergeant and voted to convert the kingdom of Italy into a republic.

7. The allies started the invasion of Sicily on July 10th and the news was widely reported by Australian newspapers. For example, the front page of Perth's *The Mirror* included an article titled "Allies Pound, then Invade Sicily".

Badoglio was the old-guard general who replaced Mussolini as prime minister.

8. All POWs in Cowra were issued identity cards with front and side pictures and finger prints.

9. Italy signed an unconditional surrender, as widely reported by the Australian press. See for example *The Morgen Bulletin* of September 10th, which included a first-page article titled "Capitulation of Italy – Allied Demand for Unconditional Surrender Accepted".

The somewhat ambiguous radio announcement made by prime minister Badoglio on the evening of September 8th (see appendix G) was going to have serious consequences for the Italian armed forces through the confusion it created.

10. At the time of the Japanese mass breakout from Cowra, on 5 August 1944, the compound commandant was Lt. Col. Montague Brown. I am not sure whether Montague Brown was already in command in 1943.

The Italian capitulation had taken the Allies by surprise, and Americans and British disagreed on what to do with the hundreds of thousands of Italian POWs they held all over the world. See Appendix H for more details.

11. Timms was the author of 22 novels, many short stories, and innumerable plays. During WWI, with the rank of lieutenant, he took part in the Gallipoli landing of 25 April 1925, where he was wounded.

12. Between 16 February 1942 and 12 November 1943, the Japanese conducted 97 air raids over northern Australia.

13. This train trip is speculation on my part. The road distance beween Cowra and the destination I have chosen for Roccafiorita (Glen Innes, in northern NSW) is approximately 700km. There was a good network of railway lines around Sydney, and I expect that Roccafiorita changed twice before travelling on the Northern Line that would take him to Glen Innes.

Glen Innes was the location of PWCC N-11 (where the N stood for NSW). PWCCs managed the POWs and assigned them to the farmers who had requested help. There were 96 Control Centres. You will find their list in Appendix D.

Glen Innes – Wednesday 15 December 1943

When Roccafiorita reached Cavanaugh farm, he was told to put his things in an old barn, where he would sleep until a better place for him could be set up. The owner, Kevin Cavanaugh, a large man with thinning red hair and an easy laugh, appeared to be apologetic that he couldn't offer anything better. But Roccafiorita didn't mind at all. He liked the smell of hay and the creaks and pops of the old wood at any gust of wind. (1)

The farmhouse was a large, flat brick building surrounded on three sides by a large veranda. Kevin's wife was waiting at the entrance door and, as soon as she saw him, she smiled at him and said "I am Colleen. Wash your hands, love. We are ready for tea." (2)

But when he came back to the farmhouse, instead of finding the tea pots and biscuits he expected, he was directed towards a table full of food. A moment later, before he could fully adjust to the unexpected situation, he was sitting at the table opposite a thin teen-ager with pimples on his face. Colleen and Kevin sat at the two ends of the long table, with four chairs left unoccupied. In the middle were two serving plates, one heaped with lamb chops and one with potatoes cooked in their jacket. (3)

The Cavanaughs folded their hands and bowed their heads. The simple gesture brought back to Roccafiorita memories of his grandfather, who never missed saying grace before a meal. He joined them with an unexpected feeling of belonging, as if he were back home instead of in a far and strange land. Kevin said in a low voice "Dear Lord, bless this food and look after those who cannot be with us today. Amen."

After that, Colleen leapt up from her chair and served everyone an abundant portion. Roccafiorita noticed that his hosts spread butter on the potatoes and spooned a thick brown sauce on top of the mutton. He did the same, and was surprised to discover that the sauce was in fact apple puree. He found that the fresh taste of crushed apples balanced the fat of the meat and suddenly realised he was famished. "This is very good Colleen. Thank you," he said between mouthfuls of food.

She smiled again. "I can see that you like it. What do we call you?"

The military had told his name to Kevin, and Roccafiorita had assumed that everybody knew it. "I apologise for not introducing myself. My name is Rosario Roccafiorita."

"You mean like the Holy Rosary?"

"Well, yes. We are all Catholics in Italy, and Sicily, where I come from, is particularly religious."

"If you are all Catholics, why did you ally yourselves with Hitler and the Japs? They are murderers and criminals," blurted the young man with a rage that he clearly found difficult to contain.

Kevin's reaction was immediate. "Patrick! Where are your manners. Apologise at once."

Roccafiorita raised his hand in an appeasing gesture. "No. It is OK. You are right Patrick. We should have never done that. Many of us didn't want it but had no choice."

And then, Roccafiorita put together the empty chairs around the table and Kevin's grace and understood what had caused Patrick's outburst. "Do you have brothers in the war?" he asked looking at the boy.

It was Kevin who replied to Roccafiorita's question. "Yes. Brendan, the eldest, and Eamon are both in the army, somewhere in Europe."

Roccafiorita wanted to say something, but couldn't come up with anything. Two young men of this family were risking their lives to free his country, while he was sitting here in their place. What could he possibly say that wouldn't sound lame? He nodded slowly and resumed eating.

The farm extended over 20,000 acres of pasture on which Merino sheep and Hereford cattle roamed free. Roccafiorita worked hard, as if to repay the simple hospitality of the Cavanaugh. Although he didn't want to admit it to himself, he also felt somewhat responsible for taking away Brendan and Eamon from their family. Broadly speaking, there are two types of people: those who shirk any responsibility and see every privilege as due to them, and those who take nothing for granted and feel responsible for what happens around them. Roccafiorita undoubtedly belonged to the latter group. Although he had had no influence on the war that was raging in Europe and, certainly, had not started it, his country was one of the aggressors, and he unconsciously felt he needed to atone for the crimes of which he had been an unwilling accomplice. (4)

Roccafiorita worked with Patrick every day. Initially, the boy didn't talk much, and Roccafiorita respected his silence. But it didn't take long for the young Australian to warm to the Italian, probably finding in him a surrogate for his brothers, whom he missed so much.

The first couple of days, Kevin came around in the morning and in the afternoon and stayed around for a few minutes before moving on. Clearly, he was checking on his new Italian farm hand. Roccafiorita didn't mind. If the roles had been reversed, he would have done the same. And he was pleased that, after a few days, Kevin stopped checking on him, and only came along when he had for him new tasks.

The evening meal at the farmhouse became for Roccafiorita the highlight of each day. He enjoyed the Cavanaughs' warmth and simple friendliness. They were curious about Italy and Sicily and, on the fourth day, they asked him to say for them the Ave Maria in Italian. They listened in silence as if he had been reciting a magic spell. When he finished, Colleen must have expressed what was on the mind of all three Cavanaughs when she said "How beautiful. It sounded like music." (5)

One week after Roccafiorita had arrived at the farm, while he and Patrick were replacing a fence post, they were interrupted by the sound of a galloping horse. It was a magnificent bay mare with black points. The rider leaned back and pulled on the reins so strongly that the animal locked its front legs, with its hooves sliding on the sparse grass. For a moment, Roccafiorita thought that it would run over him and Patrick, but it managed to stop with a metre to spare, its nostrils flaring. (6)

As soon as the dust settled, the rider bent forward on the saddle and said a few words to Patrick before flapping the reins with a quick gesture, at which the horse took off again.

Roccafiorita, who had learned how to ride a horse as soon as his feet could reach the stirrups, was impressed. "That was a beautiful horse," he said, "and the rider showed great horsemanship. Who is he?"

Patrick replied with a sonorous laugh. "He?" he said, "He is Clare, my sister!"

"That rider was a woman?"

"She sure was! And I have a word of advice for you: don't ever tell her that she rides like a man. You would make her angry, and that's something you should really avoid."

"How is it that I have been here for a week and I have never seen her?"

"She teaches at a primary school in Sydney and only comes home every other week-end. But now she will be here for a while because of the Christmas break."

Why did he expect Clare to be a hard woman with thick wrists and brusque manners? Was it because of the strength she had shown in controlling her horse? Or was it the warning that Patrick had made concerning her temper? No matter. He could have not been more wrong. When he went to the farmhouse for the evening meal, it was Clare who opened the door to let him in. But he didn't enter the house. As soon as he looked into her brown eyes, he froze. The spell was only broken several seconds later, when she said "You must be Rosario. I'm Clare. Please come in." He suddenly realised that he had been holding his breath, and managed an embarrassed nod before crossing the threshold.

When he sat at the table, his heart was pounding in his chest as if trying to break free of his rib cage. He dried the palms of his hands on the trousers and kept his eyes averted from the young lady sitting across the table. She was the cause of his turmoil. No doubt about it. It had never happened to him before. Or perhaps it had, when he was a teenager holding the hand of his first girl friend. But that was an eternity ago. He was a man now. What was it that made him feel like a boy? Her eyes? Her long hair the colour of copper? The skin that seem made of alabaster? *I've seen many women who were more beautiful.* he thought while taking a deep breath. *Her nose is too long and her mouth too small. Get hold of yourself or you will look like a fool!* As to confirm his fears, he caught Patrick looking at him with a light smirk on his face. *Great,* he thought before trying to concentrate on the plate of food before him, *That's exactly what I needed.*

The meal dragged on forever, or so it seemed to Roccafiorita. Fortunately, the Cavanaughs did most of the talking, happy about the upcoming Christmas they would spend together. Finally, the torture was over, they bid one another good night, and he scurried away to his corner of the creaky barn. How could this completely unknown girl drain him of all his courage? To exorcise her effect on him, he methodically examined her in his mind's eye, from the pony tail that whipped her shoulders when she turned to her slender hands, from the light freckles on her nose and cheeks to the graceful way she moved her lithe body. He suddenly realised that he had a powerful erection. He felt embarrassed. *But why?* he asked himself. Perhaps how he felt was just the result of the long abstinence that the army and the captivity had forced on him. *That must be it*, he thought in a futile attempt to reassure himself. *I don't know anything about her. It cannot possibly be anything else.* All he knew was that he would have gladly given away a year of his life to be able to hold her against him and caress her head buried against his neck.

1. As you will see, somewhat for fun but without intending to be disrespectful in any way, I gave to the whole Cavanaugh family common Irish names and stereotypical Irish traits.

2. The purpose of a veranda is to keep the house cooler by screening its walls and windows from direct sun. Therefore, verandas (in the southern hemisphere) usually are not built on the southern side, despite the fact that during summer the sun rises southeast and sets southwest.

3. Traditionally, Australian working-class people call the main evening meal "tea". In Sicily, Roccafiorita had been in contact with upper-middle class English people who would have called the evening meal "supper".

   In 1972, I spent one month in London as guest of an Irish family, and roasted meat with potatoes was a typical meal I shared with them.

4. 1 acre is about 4047 square metres, or 0.4 hectares. A square of 20,000 acres would have a side of approximately 9 km.

5. It is commonly accepted that Italian is a musical language (while, for example, Slavonic languages sound liquid and Germanic languages sound harsh). How a language sounds can only be fully appreciated by non-speakers of the language. But the first time I heard my wife speak

Captive Down Under

Italian to me on the phone (she is a native speaker of German), I thought *what a beautiful voice she has!*

6. Bay horses are brown, and "points" refer to mane, tail, and lower legs.

Glen Innes – Early 1944

"You like her."

"What did you say?"

"Clare. My sister. I saw how you look at her. You like her, don't you?"

Patrick was standing before Roccafiorita with the hands in his pockets. His mouth was smiling, but his eyes, fixed on Roccafiorita's, were not. Roccafiorita took the time to cross the arms on his chest before answering. "And what if I do? It is not forbidden, is it?"

"She is my sister."

"Many women are somebody's sisters."

Patrick took his hands out of the pockets and balled them on his sides. "I don't care about other people's sisters. I only care about Clare, and I don't want you to hurt her." His eyes filled with tears that he barely managed to hold back.

Roccafiorita took a step forward and placed a hand on the boy's shoulder. "Patrick, I don't want to hurt anybody. Least of all a member of the family that has accepted me like a long lost cousin. And I couldn't hurt Clare anyway. I'm just a farm hand to her. She doesn't even know I exist."

"Oh, she knows that you exist alright. I'm not blind. I see how she looks at you and averts her eyes when you turn toward her," Patrick blurted out.

Roccafiorita's heart skipped a beat. He struggled to remain outwardly calm despite the turmoil that was raging inside him. Could it be that she liked him too? He grabbed at the thin thread of hope that Patrick's words had spun and held it desperately, as if his life depended on it. And perhaps, in a sense, it did. He didn't know Clare at all. He had only exchanged a few words with her. And yet, he desperately wanted her to like him. Against any logical reason, he felt attracted to her in a way he had never experienced before.

"You are right," he told Patrick in a low voice. "I like her very much. And precisely for that reason, the last thing I want is to hurt her in any way."

Roccafiorita didn't know how to handle the situation, and lived the holiday period like a nightmare. On the one hand, he longed to be close to Clare; on the other, he avoided talking with her as much as he could, for fear of coming across like a foolish teenager. The celebrations for Christmas and New Year made his life even more difficult, as he could not simply disappear to the farthest corners of the farm. A few times, he caught Clare looking at him, but couldn't figure out whether the expression on her face was interest, curiosity, or puzzlement. She seemed to be happy to keep her distance from him, but was it really so? And what should he make of it?

Finally, she went back to Sydney and life on the farm resumed its usual routine. But Roccafiorita's mind kept running in circles and didn't find any rest. Did Clare really like him as Patrick had said? He kept thinking about it and tried to recall everything he had heard her say when he was around, but couldn't come up with anything that could confirm or deny Patrick's comment. It was maddening.

Two weeks later, Roccafiorita braced himself for Clare's return. Patrick had said that she came to the farm every other week-end. How would she behave towards him? How would he feel? Well, actually, he knew how he would feel, as his heart had started racing the moment he imagined her to be close. But when the week-end came, Clare was not there. On Saturday, while having the evening meal, Roccafiorita asked "Is Clare OK?" He had spoken in the most casual way he could muster, but felt his ears reaching the temperature of molten iron. All he could do was keep his eyes on the plate before him and hope that nobody would notice.

"Yes," said Colleen. "She said on the phone that the school has hired a new teacher and that she will spend the week-end helping her to settle in. Not to worry, you will see her again in a week."

Damn! Am I so transparent? Does everybody know that I care for her? Well, at least they don't seem to mind. He felt the heat emanating from his ears expand to his cheeks like the lava flow from the Etna, slowly but inexorably. He kept his eyes averted and all he managed to say was "Thank you." (1)

Finally, after a week that seemed never to end, Saturday arrived, and, around ten in the morning, Roccafiorita saw Clare step out of an old

Sloper, wave back to the driver, and walk toward the front porch carrying a canvas bag. He had been hovering or, better said, loitering, in the front yard for at least a couple of hours and quickly moved to intercept her before she reached the house. Despite his heart thumping all the way up to his throat, he managed to speak in a tone that some casual listeners might have even considered to be relaxed. "Good morning Clare," he started, while taking the bag from her hand, "I was wondering whether you would like to accompany me on a ride around the farm. Your father asked me to check the fence..." (2)

Only after completing his well-rehearsed piece, Roccafiorita looked up to Clare's face, and his eyes got lost in hers. She broke the spell after a brief hesitation. "Sure! I'll be happy to!" Two deep dimples formed on her cheeks as she smiled. "I love riding and it's nice to have company, but usually everybody is always too busy to ride with me. It will be fun." She looked down at her skirt. "Just give me ten minutes to change into something more comfortable." She grabbed the bag back from Roccafiorita's hand and disappeared into the house with a spring in her step.

They rode along the fence maintaining a slow trot. When they reached the farthest point from the house, Clare flicked the reins against her mount's neck and the horse took off at a light gallop. After a brief moment of surprise, Roccafiorita dug his heels into the horse's sides and followed her. Ten or fifteen seconds later, Clare stopped at the base of a low hill, tied her horse to a shrub, and climbed up the gentle slope. Roccafiorita caught up with her only when she reached the lone tree that crowned the hill. It was a majestic old eucalypt higher than a ten-storey house with a blue-grey bark and long, deep-green leaves. Its smooth trunk of at least one metre in diameter reached half the height of the tree. (3)

Clare caressed the smooth trunk of the tree with her flat hand. "Isn't it magnificent?" she asked. Then, she turned her back to the tree and leaned against it. "So Rosario, tell me."

He loved the way in which she gently rolled the Rs of his name. "Tell you what?" he said.

"That you like me.

"Or don't you?" she added with a twinkle of her eyes.

She took a step toward him while keeping her eyes locked onto his. "Patrick told me that you do."

"Are all Australian girls so forward?" he managed to say.

"Only some," she replied while taking another step. "And are all Italian men so shy?"

The scent of her hair brought to him by the breeze, made him feel light-headed, unable to think clearly. A moment later, he was wrapping his arms around her and seeking her mouth with his. It was not a gentle kiss. It was a desperate kiss, full of need. His left hand on the small of her back pushed her body hard against his, and he felt her respond to him with the same hunger, the same long-repressed desire.

When their lips finally separated, they were both breathing hard. "Only some," he said. They kissed again, slowly, savouring each other with abandon. He knew she could feel his erection, but felt no embarrassment. It was as it was supposed to be. It was as it was meant to be.

"What now?" she asked after a while.

He shook his head, as if trying it to clear it. "I like you a lot and I care about you, but we don't know each other. This could blossom into a love that will last forever or turn out to be an attraction that will wither in the space of a season."

"For the record, it is not my habit of throwing myself into the arms of the first man that happens to be at hand."

Roccafiorita laughed. "I didn't think so! And, also for the record, I saw you as somebody special from the first time we met. No other woman had ever made me feel weak in the knees as you do."

They kissed again. But then, Roccafiorita broke his embrace and took a step back while holding her hands with his. Her face was glowing as if she had been standing in front of a fireplace. And her pupils had almost completely swallowed her dark irises. In that moment, she was the most beautiful woman he had ever seen. *Is it true?* He thought. *Does she really like me?* He felt overcome by emotion, and tears welled in his eyes. *Is this how love feels?* They embraced again without saying a word.

1. Mount Etna, the tallest active volcano in Europe, is located near the eastern edge of Sicily. It is a very active volcano that erupts every few years.

2. *The Sloper* was the name of a car model that Holden introduced in 1935. It was the first *All Enclosed Coupé* built on Oldsmobile, Pontiac and Chevrolet chassis. A uniquely Australian design that was the forerunner of the modern hatchbacks.

3. A house storey is approximately 3m high.

   The eucalypt I am describing is a *Eucalyptus tereticornis*, commonly known as blue or grey gum. According to the florabank, a mature tree of this species can reach a height of 50m.

Glen Innes – 1944-1945

Two weeks later, on Clare's next return from Sydney, they stood again under the old gum and again kissed with a passion that shortened their breath. Their desire for each other was an invisible presence that electrified every touch. But their sense of respect and honour prevented them from abdicating their control to sexual attraction.

They sat down side by side with their backs against the old gum, and Rosario encircled her shoulders with his arm, drawing her close to him.

"Tell me about you," asked Clare searching his eyes with hers.

Rosario's well practised reserve took over at once. "What do you want to know?" He asked in return, somewhat brusquely.

She smiled. "Rosario, don't be defensive with me. You don't need to be. You know I like you. I like you a lot. And I like how you kiss." She smiled again. "But what do I know about you? What do I know about your world?"

He took a deep breath and rested his head aginst the smooth trunk of the tree, his eyes lost on the plain before them. "It is not easy for me to talk about myself. Perhaps it has to do with the fact that Sicily is a very conservative place, in which men are only supposed to show masculine strength, like roosters in a pen. Men talk about what they do, not what they feel, and especially not with women."

He turned to look at her. "I have never been comfortable with that, but I learnt to keep my guard up, to hide any emotion that could be interpreted as a sign of weakness."

"Are you very religious?" She asked.

"Why do you ask?"

"Because I want to know."

"And you, are you very religious?"

"I asked first," she said defiantly.

He laughed. "We are a funny couple, aren't we? So hard-headed and not wanting to give anything away."

She surprised him with her reply. "Hey, I didn't know we were a couple. Are we one? Is it official?"

They smiled at each other, both revelling in their verbal skirmishes. Rosario was the first to speak. "Of course we are a couple. You know, I think I love you."

Her eyes were shining when she replied. "You think?" She said, teasing him. Then, before he could say a word, she took his head between her hands and gently kissed him. For a moment, his entire universe was concentrated on the soft contact of her lips on his, and a shiver ran down his spine.

"So," she said pushing him back, "how religious are you?"

A deep sigh heaved his chest. "Not very much. My mother went to Mass every Sunday, but my father always had things he needed to attend to that would prevent him from accompanying her. I always went to church with my mother when I was a boy but, as I grew up, I drifted away from Mass. I respect the moral values of Christianity, but I don't know whether God exists or not. What I do believe is that good and evil are real, and try to be as good as I can.

"There," he continued after a brief pause, "now you know. Do I pass?"

"With flying colours!" She said. "I am an agnostic like you and couldn't possibly relate to either a firm believer or an heretic. That's why I needed to know. When I was a small child, I believed in everything, including Santa Claus and the Easter Bunny. Later, when I entered school, the only survivor in my pantheon of super-human beings was God, but twelve years of Catholic schools cured me of that. The nuns, instead of being models of Christian values, turned out to be rather petty and vindictive. And how they scurried around the priest who came to celebrate Mass, clucking and waving their large bottoms like hens in heat! But the final straw was when the priest who taught religion classes started calling some of us behind his desk and grabbing our buttocks. What God would allow that?"

Sitting under the old gum became a fortnightly ritual, every time Clare came back to the farm for the week-end. They spent hours telling their stories and enjoying being close. One thing was clear: what they had was not an attraction that would wither in the space of a season.

During the evening meals, Clare and Rosario behaved as was to be expected of a farm hand and the daughter of the farm owner, but their forced formality didn't fool anyone. Patrick often rolled his eyes at their efforts, while Colleen kept smiling non-stop and Kevin found any possible way to keep his attention focussed on something else.

One evening, when Clare was not at home, Kevin walked to the front veranda and asked Rosario to join him. "You know," he said when they were seated side by side on the front steps, "the girl deserves. What are your intentions?" (1)

Rosario swallowed hard. "Sir, I'm glad you bring up this subject..." At which point Kevin exploded in a loud laugh. "You don't need to Sir me son. Relax. If I didn't like you, you would have already received your marching orders to go to some other farm as far as possible from mine."

Before Rosario could reply, Kevin continued. "Clare has had a fairly sheltered life and is more vulnerable than girls who've grown up in big cities."

While maintaining a serious expression on his face, Rosario had to smile inside at the way in which Clare had approached him on the hill a few weeks back. *Here, like in Italy, fathers are always the last ones to realise that their little girls have grown up!* "Kevin," he said, "I care about Clare, and the more I get to know her the more I think that we are made for each other. I am at times hot-headed and impulsive, but I respect Clare and your family too much to do anything that I would regret later. You know I was brought up in a Catholic family, and for a Sicilian there is nothing more important than honour." (2)

"You are serious then."

"Of course I'm serious! I love her."

"Rosario, I know you are a good man, and if the circumstances were different, I would be completely happy with you courting my daughter. But we are in a war. What future can you offer her? You are a prisoner here and in a few years, or perhaps even in a few months, you will go back to your country. You will break her heart."

Rosario felt a wave of blood flow to his cheeks and struggle, with limited success, to keep his voice calm. "Who says that I will have to go back? This is a vast country and there will be work for me after the war."

Kevin was nodding, but was not finished yet. "And what about your family back in Italy? Are you going to abandon them?"

"I wish that Australia were not so far from my country. I will miss my family, but my parents have had their lives, and I must be able to have mine. There is only one future for me, and it is with Clare."

Not long after Kevin's conversation with Rosario, the radio reported that the Allies, with their slow progress up the Italian peninsula, had freed Rome. Two days after that, on the other side of the Third Reich, Allied troops landed in Normandy. In his peaceful environment, Rosario received news of the Allied successes with mixed feelings. On the one hand, he was happy that the Nazis were being pushed back on all fronts. On the other hand, he felt a deep resentment that he was not allowed to join the forces fighting to free his home country. (3)

But that was how the things were, and life on the farm proceeded unchanged, as if the fighting on the other side of the world didn't exist.

Clare and Rosario spent together as much time as they could, and their relationship grew with every hour they managed to be close to each other. They learnt of their youth and friends, of their hopes and fears, of their dreams and nightmares. And they learnt of their shared love for Rudyard Kipling and Herman Melville. They seemed to find always new things to say but, sometimes, they simply enjoyed each other's company without saying a word, happy to walk hand in hand or sit under the old gum.

It was under that old tree, in the heat of early summer 1944, that Rosario, lost in her eyes, finally said what he had been thinking for months. "Clare, dear, dear Clare, I love you more than I thought possible. I want to spend the rest of my life with you. Will you marry me?"

Her eyes filled with tears. "Where is the ring?" she asked.

He opened his mouth as if to speak but didn't say a word. She broke into a bright smile. "But of course I will marry you! I'm madly in love with you, and you know it! You silly Billy. What took you so long?" Her hands went to the back of his head and pulled him to her welcoming lips.

That night, after dinner, Rosario asked Kevin permission to marry Clare. He felt confident that Kevin would approve, but a residual worry fluttered in an undefined place between his chest and his stomach. He knew that Kevin liked him and had expressed his sympathy for him in many occasions. Still, sympathy is one thing; but letting a foreigner with a funny name take his only daughter away is something else entirely. After all, what did Kevin know about him?

"Kevin," he started. And stopped there.

"Rosario," Kevin replied, with half a smile on his lips that would have made Leonardo da Vinci proud. (4)

Kevin wasn't helping him at all. Talking to this easy-going man was turning out to be more difficult than facing the enemy in battle. But, at this point, no retreat was possible. He just had to ask his question as briefly as possible and be done with it. "Kevin, Clare and I are in love. Do we have your permission to marry?"

"MMmmm..." Kevin said, just to keep Rosario hanging. "Are you sure?"

"What question is that? Of course I'm sure! And so is Clare. If you have a problem, say it clearly!" The vein in the middle of his forehead was bulging, and his hands were balled into fists.

"Calm down, young man. I was only teasing you. You should know that I've come to consider you almost like a son. You work hard and have your head in the right place. If my daughter thinks that you are right for her, I'll be happy for you two to marry." He offered his hand to Rosario, who took it with relief. "Come," Kevin said, "let's go tell Colleen."

Colleen's reaction didn't leave any doubt on what she thought: she threw her arms around Rosario's neck and placed a sonorous kiss on each one of his cheeks.

The next time the officer in charge of the Glen Innes Control Centre visited the farm for the regular roll call of unsupervised POWs, Kevin told him that his daughter intended to marry Rosario. The officer, a middle-aged reservist who in civilian life had worked as a real-estate agent, cleared his voice before replying in a conspiratorial tone. "Mr. Cavanaugh, I will forget what you just told me, and I suggest that you keep it for yourself. Fraternising with the prisoners is strictly forbidden and attracts fines of up to £100, six months imprisonment, or both. In fact, very recently, a woman from Adelaide was fined £50 because she was having an affair with an Italian prisoner and expressed the intention of marrying him." (5)

"But that is absurd! The Italians are no longer our enemies, are they? I would understand it if Rosario were German or Japanese, but Italian... What should two young people in love do?"

"Wait for the end of the war, I suppose," the officer said.

"It shouldn't last much longer," he added with a bland smile before turning on his heels and walking away.

Clare was devastated, while Rosario could barely contain his anger. It didn't make any sense. (6)

"What are we going to do?" asked Clare with a tremor in her voice.

Rosario unballed his fists and put his arm around her shoulders. "We go ahead. Once we are married, the authorities will have to accept it."

"But don't we need an authorisation to marry? And what about the banns? If our intention to marry is announced at the parish for three consecutive Sundays, somebody will tell the authorities. You know that many are against Italian POWs working in the community. They will not miss the opportunity to report us."

"We must talk with Father Maurice. He will know what to do", Kevin said. (7)

On the following Sunday, the Cavanaughs and Rosario, after attending mass at St Patrick's Catholic church in Glen Innes, followed Father Maurice to the Sacristy and explained their situation. To their great relief, the priest told them that if they provided a sworn declaration and paid a moderate fee, Clare and Rosario could obtain a marriage licence without the usual notice period under the banns.

The date of the wedding was set for April 7th, the first Saturday after Easter, in the early afternoon. Given the circumstances, only few people were invited to attend the ceremony: a handful of the Cavanaughs' relatives who lived in Victoria, two neighbours, and Clare's closest friend. After the ceremony at St Patrick's, the guests would all go to the

Cavanaugh farm for an afternoon of celebration with cakes, tea, and dances. A local Irish band was engaged well in advance to play live music.

In mid March, after a couple of months of planning and organising, all that was left to do was waiting. As it often happens though, things were going to take an unexpected turn. On Monday 19th, less than three weeks before the wedding, a message from the Control Centre notified Rosario that on the following Monday, the 26th, he was going to be transferred back to Cowra in preparation for his repatriation. (8)

1. You might have noticed that I am using *deserves* without a direct object. I couldn't resist repeating here what the father of a girlfriend of mine actually told me. It was in Italian, but the intransitive usage of the verb was as odd in Italian as it is in English. At the time, my friend and I were nineteen years old. It really was another century and another culture!

2. Family honour was (and perhaps still is) very important in Italian traditional communities. Till 5 September 1981, Italian law punished the murdering of the spouse, a daughter, or a sister with only three to seven years of jail if it was motivated by safeguarding the murderer's honour. The same light penalty applied to the murder of a person who was involved in an "illicit carnal relationship with the spouse, the daughter, or the sister". Such crimes were called *delitti d'onore* (*crimes of honour*).

3. Rome was freed from German occupation on 4 June 1944.

   The landing in Normandy started on 6 June 1944. I find it interesting that these two important dates (the liberation of Rome in the South and D-day in the North), although so close to each other, are never mentioned together.

4. It should be obvious that the mentioning of Leonardo da Vinci refers to the enigmatic smile of the Gioconda.

5. The Prisoners of War Control Centres were responsible for the welfare of the POWs, and their commanding officers paid regular visits to the farms. According to the Reports on the Directorate of Prisoners of War and Internees at Army Headquarters (AWM), the Glen Innes CC,

between December 1943 and December 1945 was responsible for 100 Italian POWs.

In real life, the incident in Adelaide happened several months later, in April 1945.

6. According to the 1927 Geneva Convention on the Treatment of POWs, "the repatriation of prisoners shall be effected as soon as possible after the conclusion of peace." It was therefore not completely unreasonable to forbid marriages with prisoners, who had to be sent back to their country of origin in any case.

7. Dean Maurice Tobin was the real name of the priest in St Patrick's Parish, Glen Innes, from 9 December 1914 to 12 April 1955.

8. This transfer to Cowra on 26 March 1945 actually happened to Pietro Gargano, the prisoner who inspire me to write this story.

Glen Innes – Wednesday 21 March, 1945, early afternoon

Father Maurice dabbed at his forehead with a large handkerchief. "I cannot do that!"

Rosario was about to explode in one of his typical outbursts of emotions, but Kevin squeezed his forearm, signalling him to calm down. Perhaps there were times when shouted words and bulging eyes would be appropriate, but this was not one of them. The two men and Clare were facing the priest in the small sacristy of St Patrick's church.

"Father," Kevin said, directly looking into the priest's eyes, "you have known me for thirty years. In all these years, have you ever had any cause to think that I am an unreasonable man?"

"Of course not, Kevin. But what has that to do with..."

"It has everything to do with what I'm asking. If I knew of any alternative, I wouldn't be bothering you. But you are the only person who can help us. What difference does it make if you celebrate the wedding tomorrow instead of waiting for the seventh of April?"

The priest shook his head.

Kevin drew in a breath and continued undeterred. "There will not be a wedding on the seventh in any case. I told you, next Monday, Rosario will be sent back to a POW camp to be repatriated. You were prepared to bend the rules and celebrate the wedding without authorisation from the army. I say, let's do it tomorrow and present the authorities with a done deal. [1]

The priest looked down at the small table that stood between him and his visitors, without saying a word.

"Father, they want to be joined in matrimony, but they are also young and in love. I fear that if you refuse to consecrate their union, they will commit sin."

Rosario felt his cheeks begin to burn and heard Clare draw a sharp breath. On his part, Father Maurice snapped his head up as if he had suddenly realised that a snake had slithered into his collar. "Now, Kevin, it's not proper to talk that way."

"Then help us."

"God help us all.", said the priest with a long sigh.

The next day, on Thursday, March 22nd, Rosario and Clare became husband and wife. Clare wore her mother's wedding dress, which Colleen herself had adapted to Clare's measures. It had taken days for the smell of mothballs to dissipate. (2)

Rosario wore Brendan's only suit. Sleeves and trousers were a bit short, but it was war time, and ill-fitting clothing was almost commonplace, as people did their best with the scarce resources available. (3)

The few old ladies who happened to be in the church looked on baffled as the brief ceremony took place. When she walked out of the church, Clare had on the fourth finger of her left hand the ring that had belonged to Colleen's mother, while Rosario wore a silverish ring that the local blacksmith had made with a thin slice of a steel pipe. (4)

The following morning, Clare and Rosario took the first train to Sydney. In the big city, as a married couple and with Rosario speaking such good English, nobody could possibly suspect that he was an escaped POW.

Clare continued teaching as if nothing had happened, but took the precaution of removing her wedding ring when she went to work, so as not to elicit curiosity from their colleagues. Although, as she told Rosario, the most inquisitive and gossipy of them noticed that she was particularly happy. "They keep asking me what makes me laugh so easily, whether it is love or money. I would like to show off my handsome Sicilian husband," at which Rosario laughed, "but I don't trust them. They are the envious type and might just run directly to the police."

The war had caused factories to pop up all over the place like new friends after a lottery win, and Rosario had no problems in finding a job. He worked at building engines for the Bristol Beaufort bomber. On his first day at the factory, he had to smile, thinking that the Geneva Convention prohibited employing POWs in jobs connected to the war effort. (5)

Paradoxically, although he could be at any moment recaptured and sent behind barbed wire, Rosario felt more free than he had ever felt at home in Sicily. In Italy, everybody had to register with the municipality within a few days after moving to a new place. The police could stop everybody at any time in the middle of the street and take them to the police station if they were unable to show any form of identification. (6)

But it took Clare and Rosario months before they felt they could relax. At the beginning, they avoided public spaces as much as possible and crossed to the side of the street whenever they noticed in the distance that a policeman was moving towards them. Then, with the passing of weeks, they began thinking that they might never be found. After all, almost everybody Rosario had ever met in Australia was either in a POW camp or in a PWCC. And the police certainly had more important things to do than chasing an escaped POW who hadn't committed any crime.

Unfortunately, they had underestimated the importance that the Australian authorities placed on recapturing escaped POWs. It was no longer a matter of national security, as Italy had been at peace with Australia for a couple of years. Nevertheless, some Australians resented that the government employed POWs at less than standard wages. Others were concerned that the young Italian prisoners would take advantage of Australian women while their husbands were at war. It was therefore important for the authorities to show that they had the situation fully under control and that the POWs were kept in line. (7)

It took the slow but efficient Australian justice more than a year to catch up with Clare and Rosario. In the first hours of April 23, 1946, a loud banging on the door and a peremptory "Police! Open immediately!" threw them out of bed. (8)

As soon as Rosario opened the door, two uniformed police officers grabbed him by the arms. A third man, who was dressed in a crumpled grey suit, checked Rosario's face against a small photograph and nodded to the two officers, who handcuffed the Italian without saying a word. The man in civilian clothes, who was clearly in charge, struggling with the pronunciation of Rosario's name, asked the prisoner to confirm who he was: "Are you *Rousareeou Roccafuoritia*?"

Rosario, who had always hated to hear his name mispronounced, let his temper fly. What did have to lose anyway? "No Sir. My name is John Watson. And I don't appreciate this irruption at this ungodly hour. Take these handcuffs off me at once and get out of here. Being the police doesn't give you the right to harass law-abiding citizens." (9)

The officer in grey suit was visibly taken aback by Rosario's well-educated reply spoken in perfect English. It is not completely unreasonable to suppose that all the Italian POWs he had previously encountered could only make themselves understood in broken English. His cheeks turned a bright red and, for a moment, it appeared that Rosario's diversion might succeed.

But it was not going to be that simple. After all, Rosario was clearly the man whose face was on the picture. The officer passed the fingers of his left hand through his thinning blond hair and gave a second look at the picture he was still holding in his right. "You're a smart arse, aren't you?" he said. "First of all, you come with me to the police station.

"And you," he added after turning his eyes towards Clare, "you come too."

The proceedings at the Magistrates Court in Sydney only lasted a couple of days. The results were not surprising: Rosario was sent back to Cowra to wait repatriation, and Clare was fined £70 with additional £2 of costs. (10)

In court, it also became clear how the police had been able to track down Clare and Rosario. The army truck sent to Cavanaugh farm for Rosario on 26 March 1945 failed to pick him up because he had run away. In his report about Rosario's disappearance, the officer in charge of Glen Innes's Control Centre expressed the suspicion that a liaison between the escapee and the farmer's daughter might have been the reason for the escape. Almost one year passed before a zealous police sergeant (the man in grey), going through the files on the escapees, noticed the remark concerning Rosario. It was then easy to follow Clare from her place of work to her home. (11)

The Cavanaughs, determined to keep Rosario in Australia, instead of dealing with the police turned to the Army organisation responsible for handling the POWs. They quickly discovered that it was part of a larger operation, the Directorate of Prisoners of War and Internees at Army Headquarters (PW&I), which, beside dealing with enemy POWs, was also responsible for foreign nationals interned in Australia, war crimes, and Australian POWs. (12)

After a week lost in the labyrinthine machinery of the PW&I, Clare and Kevin were finally sitting before Capt J.K. Allison, who, they had been told, was a staff captain of the Enemy-PW Section. After listening to their story, the young captain replied with a simple "There is nothing I can do." (13)

"What?" Clare blurted out. "There is nothing you can do? Is that all you have to say?"

The captain cleared his voice before replying. "According to the 1929 Geneva Convention of which both Australia and Italy are signatories, we have to repatriate all POWs." (14)

On 30 July 1946, H.M.S. Moreton Bay sailed from Sydney with Rosario on board. (15)

1. I would have preferred to use the expression *fait accompli* instead of *done deal*, but it would have probably sounded inappropriate for a farmer of the mid 1940s to say so.

2. I couldn't find any source to confirm that mothballs were widely used during the first half of the twentieth century, but it can be safely assumed, as naphtalene, their main constituent, according to a web site entirely dedicated to mothballs, was first refined one hundred years before.

3. That often people had to put up with ill-fitting clothing is what my mother told me about war-time Italy. It seems reasonable to assume the it applied to all belligerent nations, although the situation in Italy was particularly bad because of the sanctions imposed by the League of Nations as a result of Italy's occupation of Ethiopia.

4. My father actually made his wedding ring out of a piece of steel tubing when he married my mother in April 1942 while he was serving in the Royal Italian Navy. After my father died in 1980, I had a jeweler reduce it in size to fit my finger and have been wearing it since.

5. John Wilkinson of the NSW Parliamentary Library Research Services reports that in 1945, the Australian manufactoring industry employed 751,000 people.

   The Bristol factory was the factory located at Lidcombe that the Commonwealth Aircraft Corporation built following the start of the Pacific War.

Indeed, the 1927 Geneva Convention on the Treatment of POWs stated that "Work done by prisoners of war shall have no direct connection with the operations of the war."

6. This obligation to register with the municipality of residence has been, and still is, a requirement in most, if not all, European countries. When I migrated to Australia, I was very surprised to find out that there was no ID card and that I could simply move from one place to another without telling any authority.

   During Fascism, the Black Shirts had an overpowering presence. But, still in the early 1970s in Rome, when I used to walk home after midnight from my girlfriend's place, I was stopped on several occasions by the police and asked to show the content of my bag. The 1970s were the so called "Years of Lead", when the Red Brigades kidnapped and executed politicians and the neo-fascists exploded bombs in crowded places.

7. The resentment of Australians towards POWs' cheap labour is well reported. See for example Hall's article titled "Bad Press".

   The daily press reported several incidents involving Italian POWs and Australian women. See for example the article titled "Attempt To Seduce: Italian POW Before Court" and published on the Army News, Darwin, NT, 14 July 1945.

8. 23 April 1946 was two days after Easter and two days before ANZAC Day.

   Police often perform arrests in the middle of the night, when people are more likely to be caught by surprise. I know the feeling, as a squad of half a dozen police officers once threw me out of bed at 04:00 AM. A friend of mine whom I was hosting for a while had given my telephone number to a friend of hers who turned out to be a Red Brigadist. When the police arrested him and found my telephone number, they thought that I was the head of a terrorist cell!

9. John Watson is the full name of Sir Arthur Conan Doyle's character that everybody simply knows as "Dr. Watson." Roccafiorita liked to read Sherlock Holmes novels.

Roccafiorita uses the unusual term *irruption* to take the police officers off balance. While *irruzione* is very common in Italian, the English equivalent, due to its Latin origin, sounds somewhat haughty. And I believe that *ungodly* is another "well educated" word.

10. I believe a fine of 70 pounds to be commensurate to the charges, as a woman was charged in Adelaide £50 plus costs for stating to the police that her relationship with an Italian POW "was a love affair and she intended to marry him after the war."

11. For your information, the Glen Innes PWCC was closed in December 1945 (see Appendix D), after all the POWs had been moved to camps.

The officer knew of the intended marriage but had not reported it. It is reasonable to assume that he felt somewhat responsible for Roccafiorita's escape and tried to redress his dereliction of duty by mentioning the relationship in his report.

12. AWM. The Directorate was such a complex organisation that it included a coordination Section.

13. I have in fact no idea about the age of Capt Allison.

14. I don't actually know whether Capt Allison was a man but, given the time and place, it is reasonably safe to assume that he was.

Both Australia and Italy signed the Geneva Convention of 27 July 1929; Italy ratified it on 24 March 1931 and Australia on 23 June 1931. Japan also signed the treaty on 27 July 1929, but it never ratified it.

In 1947, the Apostolic Delegate in Australia intervened, and the Minister for Immigration allowed the few remaining escapees to marry Australian women and remain in Australia. But it was too late for our hero.

15. The ocean liner S.S. Moreton Bay, built in 1921 for the Australian Commonwealth Line, was converted to armed merchant cruiser in 1939.

The ship left Sydney with 172 Italian POWs and stopped in Fremantle on August 6th to pick up further 327 prisoners.

H.M.S. Moreton Bay – August 1946

Rosario rested his forearms on the railing and looked out at the sea, his mind lost in the events of the past five and a half years. Despite the many dull months spent in camps or working on the railway, it had been a wild ride, an emotional rollercoaster.

Clare alone had given him a whole lifetime of emotions in a couple of years: surprise, attraction, hope, love, expectation, happiness. And just when he felt on top of the world, the inexorable military machinery had crushed him like the lava flow from Etna, slow but unstoppable. Perhaps there was a God and this was his way of teaching him a lesson of humility. (1)

He had only been at sea for a week and already missed her passionate embrace as if a vital organ had been wrenched away from his body. Kevin was going to sponsor his return to Australia, but who knows how many months or years it would take before he would be back?

The ship had just left Fremantle, where it had stopped to pick up Italian POWs being repatriated from Western Australia. This return journey was going to take much longer than his first crossing of the Indian Ocean aboard the Queen Mary. Perhaps, it was better so. It would give him time to prepare for the reunion with his family. He was looking forward to see his mother again, but he also knew that his marriage in Australia and his desire to leave Italy would be a shock for her. (2)

A loud and familiar voice jolted him out of his dark thoughts. "Signor Tenente!"

When he turned, he was welcomed by the warm smile of corporal Pol. They embraced like long-lost brothers. Pol took a step back and scanned Roccafiorita from head to toes. "You look well, Sir. This prolonged holiday has done you good!" (3)

Roccafiorita grinned. "It seems that you also benefited from the Australian resorts! You look thinner." Then, looking up to Pol's head, "And your hair looks thinner too!" (4)

He stretched out his right hand. "After all we have gone through, don't you think that we should dispense with ranks and formalities? Please, call me Rosario, or, better still, call me Saro, like my family and close friends."

The corporal hesitated. "Oh, I don't know whether I'll be able to do that, S..." He laughed. "But I'll try. And you must call me Bepi," he continued while firmly clasping the offered hand. (5)

Pol's life in Australia had been much less adventurous than Roccafiorita's. After Italy had surrendered to the allies, he had been sent to help with loading and unloading ships in Sydney's harbour. Having cultivated corn in Veneto for most of his life, he convinced the officer in charge of his Control Centre to send him to one of the large corn farms in WA, where he had remained till repatriation. (6)

It was a great relief for Rosario to have somebody he could talk with. Sharing his pain with Pol seemed to make it a little more bearable, perhaps because the corporal, having been separated from his fiancée for six years, understood how Rosario felt.

"I'm sure you could have escaped again. The surveillance was not as strict as when we arrived. Why didn't you?"

"Ah Bepi, till the last minute I hoped that they would let me stay. I couldn't believe that they would separate husband and wife. (7)

"But you, have you considered migrating to Australia after marrying your fiancée? It is a young country where a man can easily make a good life for himself and his family."

Pol didn't need to reflect before replying. He clearly had given to the idea some serious thoughts. "I know. If I were alone, I think I would go back. But Rosina comes from a traditional family and is very attached to her brothers and sisters. I couldn't possibly take her away to the other side of the world. It would break her heart." (8)

Saro and Bepi spent the weeks at sea talking. Before being thrown together into the cauldron of the North African campaign, they had had completely different lives and experiences. Their dialects, which were the best way they had for expressing their thoughts and feelings, were so different from each other that they might as well have been foreign languages. Even when speaking in Italian, they used sometimes words and idioms that they needed to explain. They also knew that, once back in Italy, their paths would diverge, probably forever. But they were good men who had gone through hell together and were now facing an uncertain future. Their differences seemed insignificant.

It was an emotional moment when they crossed the Suez Canal. Knowing that they were sailing on the Mediterranean made them already feel at home. This was their sea. (9)

And then, finally, almost one month after leaving Australia, they arrived in Naples. When they stepped onto the pier, no bands or delegations welcomed them home. Instead, they were hastily corralled towards an office where they would get their travel documents to go home. They were still in the army, but it was a different one, and the demobilisation could wait. (10)

It took Rosario days to reach his family in Sicily. The train stopped at times for hours in the middle of nowhere, and when it passed through a town, it was sometimes surrounded by ruins. They were the places where the advancing allies had to fight their way against the German army street by street. Brick and stone houses that had withstood for centuries earthquakes and floods had been reduced to rubble by the merciless pounding of cannons and mortars.

What stories of suffering and loss were buried under the ruins? And how long was it going to take to reconstruct those villages?

Through the smeared window beside his wooden, 3rd class seat, Rosario saw a lot of misery. Sometimes he saw men standing along the railway line as if in a daze, battered hat low on their foreheads and hands pressed in their trousers pockets. Everybody looked so thin. (11)

On the ferry across the Strait of Messina, he stepped off the train and looked at the approaching coastline of Sicily. The air was cold and heavy with saltiness, but he didn't mind. He was finally going back home.

And yet, this return was not like he had thought it would be. For years, while surrounded by barbed wire or working on the East-Weat Railway in the dusty heat of the Nullarbor Plain, his family's home was like a piece of paradise on earth, a spring of fresh water in the middle of a desert. But now, every step that took him closer to home, also dragged him away from his love. Without Clare at his side, this return seemed meaningless.

A young man walked to the railing a couple of metres away from where Rosario was standing and, like him, looked at the approaching land, lost in his thoughts. Rosario suddenly felt the need to talk with another human being, perhaps in a vain attempt to fill the void he felt inside him. "Going home?" He asked turning towards the other man and resting an elbow on the railing.

The young man looked at Rosario and nodded. "Yes," he said.

Rosario took a step towards him and offered his hand. "Roccafiorita, Rosario," he said.

The man shook Rosario's hand firmly, and only then Rosario realised how thin the man was. His hand felt like bones and skin, and his cheeks were like holes on the sides of his face. "Barone, Salvatore," the man said. (12)

"I was a prisoner in Australia for seven years," Rosario said.

Salvatore look at him intensely before replying. "It's a long time, but they must have treated you well. I was also a prisoner, but of the Germans. Thanks God it was only for a year. I would have not survived another six months. Many didn't make it as long as I did." (13)

When the ferry docked in Messina, the two men walked back to the train and entered the same compartment. The carriage was second class, but an official-looking page with 'III' in big letters had been glued to its doors. The seats were more comfortable than in third-class carriages, and they had the compartment for themselves, perhaps because other passengers had not realised that the carriage had been declassed. As soon as they got on board, as if they had exchanged a telepathic message, they stowed their bags in the overhead racks and laid on the two facing rows of seats. They both looked at the panelled ceiling and remained quiet for a long while, reflecting on what they had gone through and what the future could bring. (14)

The railway line skirted the northern coast of Sicily on its way to Palermo, where they would change train. Rosario was going to take a local train towards the interior, while Salvatore would travel on along the coast to Trapani. Although the distance between Messina and Palermo was not much more than 200 km, the men knew that the journey would take several hours.

Rosario, lulled by the rhythmic sound of the wheels bumping on rail joints, drifted into a state in which he was neither asleep nor awake. He was suddenly called back to full wakefulness by Salvatore. "So," the young man said, "how is Australia?" (15)

"Big," replied Rosario, "so big that Italy would fit in it dozen times. And dry, with little water and a lot of deserts. But there is also a lot of land that can be cultivated. I know. I worked on a farm for two years, and it was enormous." (16)

"On a farm?"

"Yes, on a farm. Many Italian prisoners worked on farms. Probably thousands. I'm not sure". (17)

"Plenty of work then?"

"Plenty. Australia is almost empty, and the Australians are desperate for people to migrate to their country. One of the government minister even said 'Populate or perish'." (18)

"A growing nation, space, and work. It sounds too good to be true.

"And how are the Australian girls?" Salvatore added with a dreamy smile.

Rosario laughed. "I was waiting for you to come to that. The Australian girls are like girls everywhere: some are ugly or silly, but there are others who are beautiful and smart. And I know what I'm talking about. I married one of them!"

Salvatore sat up so quickly that he almost fell off his seat. "You did what? You married an Australian girl?"

"I did."

"And what *minchia* are you doing here?" (19)

"They forced me back and didn't let her come with me."

"*Figli di puttana* (*Sons of bitches*)! And what are you going to do?"

"Beside cursing them and writing letters to my wife, you mean? I will go back as soon as I can, of course. But it might take years." (20)

"Do you think that they would take me as well?" Salvatore asked after a brief hesitation. (21)

Rosario looked at him as if reflecting on what to answer. "Well, you would have to put on some weight first. And you might like to learn a few words of English. But why not?"

Instead of commenting on what Rosario had said, Salvatore asked "Do you have a picture of your wife?"

Rosario, without saying a word, took the small picture of Clare that he kept in his wallet and gave it to Salvatore, who looked at her with the eyes wide open. When he returned it a few seconds later, he said "She is very beautiful. She looks like an American actress." Which, from his tone, seemed to be the biggest compliment that one could make about a woman's appearance.

"She does," Rosario whispered while putting back the picture into his wallet, with a care that most people would have reserved for the relic of a saint.

When the train reached *Palermo Centrale* and the two men stepped onto the platform, they were surrounded by the heavy breathing of idling steam locomotives and the acrid smoke of burning coal. They briefly embraced and walked in opposite directions, towards their uncertain futures.

Hours later, after one more journey on a train that seemed to spend more time stopped than rolling, Rosario reached the closest railway station to his town. Then, he boarded an olive green bus with a white star on the door. When he stepped off the bus, his family's home was less than half an hour of walk on an unsealed road. (22)

As soon as Rosario's mother saw his son approaching the house, she raced to him and launched herself into his arms with such an impetus that she almost knocked him over. "*Figghiu miu, turnasti!*" (23)

Later, around the dinner table, Rosario finally found the courage to say what had been on his mind since he had left Australia. There was no point in trying to sugar coat it, and Rosario blurted out everything in a single sentence. "Mother, in Australia I got married and I will go back there as soon as I can."

"You got married?" was all Rosario's mother could say. And the rest of the family stared at him, like rabbits dazed by the high beams of a car.

In response, Rosario raised his left hand to show the wedding ring and then fished out of his wallet the small picture showing Clare's smiling face. (24)

His mother took the picture from his hand and looked at it for several seconds before commenting. "She looks like an angel," she said. And it was a fair description, as Clare's hair had caught the light and looked like a halo around her head.

"She doesn't look like an angel, mother. She is an angel, and I love her very much."

Rosario had expected her mother to scream and tear her hair at the idea of once more losing him. But he should have known better. When she raised her eyes from the picture and looked at him, she said: "You know, a mother never ceases to see in her children the babies that they once were. So, for me you will always be my little boy that I would like to keep attached to my skirt. But what really matters is that you are happy, even if you will be far away. I will cry when you will leave, but you must live your life. What mother would I be if I tried to hold you back?" (25)

It took Rosario more than a year to obtain the visa to return to Australia. The twenty-eight days spent aboard the Italian ship *Napoli*, of the Achille Lauro's fleet, seemed never to end. (26)

Finally, the Sydney Harbour Bridge appeared in full view before him. It looked more beautiful than when he had first seen it from the deck of the Queen Mary as a prisoner of war. But his patience was sorely tested, as it still took hours to dock, disembark, and go through the immigration procedure. (27)

When he finally emerged from customs, Rosario anxiously scanned the crowds of people waiting for relatives and friends. What if Clare had not been able to make it? He felt he couldn't wait a second longer to hold her in his arms. But then he saw her walking towards him, and his heart skipped a beat. At last, they were again together. Now, nobody would ever take them apart again.

He kissed her tenderly, and then looked down at the bundle she was holding in her arms. "You could have told me," he said. "I assume she is mine?"

"Of course not. I just borrowed her from a friend to give you a shock."

They both laughed.

THE END

1. Unstoppable is correct, but Italian engineers have learned how to divert the flow of lava away from inhabited areas. Although, I suspect that it was first successfully done well after the events being narrated in this story.

2. The Queen Mary could sustain a speed of 28 knots, while the maximum speed of the Moreton Bay was 15 knots (as reported on Wikipedia for its twin ship Jervis Bay).

3. That Pol was transferred from NSW to WA is not realistic. As far as I know, all POWs held in WA were directly disembarked in Fremantle. But I wanted Roccafiorita and Pol to meet again without having to board the ship together in Sydney. In any case, such an encounter requires some suspension of disbelief, as 3,500 prisoners were employed in Western Australian farms (see Appendix D) but only 327, or less than 10%, boarded the Moreton Bay in August 1946.

   There is nothing that brings two men closer together than having faced death side by side.

4. This is a poetic licence of mine, as the Italian translation of *thin* is *snello* when it refers to a body and *radi* when it refers to hair (ending with *i* instead of *o* because in Italian the word for hair is plural). Therefore, such comment would be impossible in Italian. When I'll translate this story into Italian, I'll have a problem here.

5. Switching from a formal address to an informal one is more difficult in Italian than in modern English, because the person of verbs also changes, from the third feminine person (*lei*, equivalent to *she* in

English, also used when talking with men) to the second person (*tu*, equivalent to the English *thou*). Traditionally, the pronoun used when addressing a person respectfully was *voi* (equivalent to the plural *you* of English), which is still used today in some areas of Southern Italy. All his life, my father addressed my mother's mother with *voi*, although he called her *mamma* (*mom*).

6. This paragraph is designed to make Pol's transfer to WA somewhat plausible. I have never read anywhere that POWs did that type of work.

7. In 1947, the few Italian escapees still at large were allowed to marry and remain in Australia. As far as I could ascertain, only a single prisoner was repatriated leaving his Australian wife behind. That POW must have been the father of a friend of mine, who married in early November 1946 while at large, surrendered one week later to the authorities, and was repatriated on 10 January 1947. He then returned to Australia as a migrant in mid January 1949. His story is what inspired my to write *Captive Down Under*.

8. Bepi Pol was the name of my father's mother's brother. He and his wife Rosina were farmers in the Veneto region and took my father in when he was three years old, after my grandmother had died of Spanish flu. I chose these names to pay homage to them.

   The only published estimate of the number of Italian POWs who, after repatriation, returned to Australia as migrants is 1,700, or 9.4% of the total (O'Connor, Desmond, 2003).

9. Indeed, the Romans called the Mediterranean *Mare Nostrum*, which is Latin for *Our Sea*.

10. On 2 June 1946, the majority of Italians had voted in a national referendum to abandon the monarchy. Therefore, the word *Regio* (i.e., *Royal*) had been removed from *Regio Esercito* (i.e., *Royal Army*), and the emblem of the royal family had disappeared from the middle of the Italian Flag. The 2nd day of June is still celebrated today as the *Anniversario della Repubblica*, with a huge military parade running in Rome from the Colosseum to Piazza Venezia.

11. My mother used to tell me that, after the end of the war, you would be hard pressed to find a fat person on the street!

12. Salvatore Barone was a colleague and a friend when I served in the Italian Army as a second leutenant. He was from Sicily and I like to remember him by using his name in this story. I am confident that, if he will ever read Captive Down Under, he will not mind to see his name in print!

13. My father's brother was deported to Germany after Italy signed a separate peace with the allies, and only managed to survive because he worked in the kitchen. When he went back home, his weight was about 30 kg.

14. While American trains were from the very beginning organised with two rows of seats on both sides of a long aisle, European trains were for many years divided in compartments containing eight seats each. Before the introduction of a corridor on one side, the compartments were completely separated from each other. This meant that the checking of tickets was impossible, and that the passengers could only visit a lavatory when the train stopped at a station.

It was common practice in the Italian Railways to declass carriages when there was a shortage of the the appropriate type or when carriages were of an older model and about to be decommissioned. I remember using a second-class ticket to travel on thickly-upholstered seats covered with velvet in compartments full of mirrors.

I slept on declassed carriages many times during my military service, travelling between Pisa (where I was posted) and Rome to spend the week-end with my girlfriend. As an officer, I didn't need to remain at the barracks unless I was on duty.

15. Nowadays, rail tracks are welded together but, up to at the time, all segments of tracks were jointed together with perforated steel plates and bolts. The gaps between segments left to prevent heat expansion to cause buckling of the rails resulted in the 'clickety-clack' sound that many people are still familiar with.

16. Actually, Australia's total area is 7,692,024 km^2, while the area of Italy is 301,338 km^2, twenty-five and a half times smaller.

17. After the end of the war, the Directorate of Prisoners of War and Internees at Army Headquarters reported that as at 22 June, 1944, 8,475

Italian POWs were employed in the rural industry (AWM, Volume 1, Part 3, Chapter 1, p 229).

18. According to the Australian Bureau of Statistics, at the end of June 1947, Australia had a population of 7,580,820.

The minister was Arthur Calwell, Minister for Immigration in Ben Chifley's Labor government from 1945 to 1947.

19. As I already explained elsewhere, *minchia*, the Sicilian word for *cock*, is used by men to emphasise surprise. But, as it can be imagined, it should never be used in polite conversation!

20. I have estimated that it took an average of two years for Italian POWs to complete the necessary paperwork.

21. Anecdotal evidence suggests that repatrieated POWs played an important role in making friends and relatives aware of the opportunities that they might find in Australia. It would be interesting to explore this possibility with rigorous historical and sociological research.

22. Vehicles of the United States Army always had white stars painted on their sides. I am suggesting here that American decommissioned buses were used for local transport in post-war Italy. I don't know whether this happened, but it seems reasonable to assume that the invading (as well as the retreating) armies left behind pieces of equipment that the local villagers managed to put to good use.

23. Speaking in Sicilian dialect, Roccafiorita's mother says *Figlio mio, sei tornato!*, which means *My son, you have returned!* Notice how in the Sicilian dialect, *figlio* becomes *figghiu*, the perfect tense of *sei tornato* becomes the past tense *tornasti*, and *o* becomes a *u*. This gives you an idea of how different the Italian dialects can be from the Florentine language that has been adopted as standard Italian.

24. Obviously, it was a black and white photo.

25. This is what my mother told me when I migrated to Australia.

26. A passenger ship named Napoli sailed in 1948 from Naples to Melbourne via Port Said, Colombo, and Freemantle. I don't know whether it ever sailed to Sydney, but I liked the idea that the name of

the ship was identical to the Italian name of the port of departure. As a curiosity, in 1948, a third-class ticket from Italy to Australia cost approximately 238,000 lire, which, on the basis of historical inflation, corresponded to more or less 4,500 of today's Euros. Not a cheap voyage. At that time, Britons who migrated to Australia only paid £10, equivalent to £377 in today's money.

27. I have adapted the two sentences about Sydney Harbour from Rick Pisaturo's book *Australia, My Love* (p 84).

Appendix A
War Declaration, Rome 10 June 1940

The following text is the translation into English I made directly from the original video-clip of the speech.

Fighters of the land, sea, and air! Blackshirts of the revolution and of the legions! Men and women of Italy, the Empire and the Kingdom of Albania! Hearken!

A fateful hour tolls in the sky of our fatherland (Enthusiastic cheers). This is the hour of the irrevocable decisions. The declaration of war has already been delivered (cheers, loud cries of "War! War!") to the ambassadors of Great Britain and France. We take the field against the plutocratic and reactionary democracies of the West, which have always hindered the march, and often threatened the very existence, of the Italian people.

Several years of the most recent history can be summarised in the words promises, threats, and blackmail and, in the end, as a crowning of the whole edifice, the ignoble concerted siege of fifty-two states.

We have absolute peace of conscience (Applause). Together with you, the whole world is witness that the Italy of the Littorio has done everything humanly possible to avoid the storm that upsets Europe, but all was in vain.

It would have been enough to revise the treaties in order to adapt them to the changing needs of the life of nations, rather than to consider them untouchable for eternity; it would have been enough not to start the foolish policy of the guarantees, which has revealed itself above all deadly for those who have accepted it; it would have been enough not to reject the proposal that the Führer made on October 6 last year, after completing the Polish campaign.

All that now belongs to the past. If today we are determined to face the risks and sacrifices of a war, it is because our honour, our interests, and our future firmly dictate it, as a great nation is truly great [only] if it considers its commitments as sacred and if it does not escape the supreme tests that determine the course of history.

After resolving the problem of our continental borders, we take up arms to solve the problem of our sea borders; we want to break the territorial and military chains that choke us in our sea, as a people of forty-five million souls is not truly free if it doesn't have free access to the Ocean.

This gigantic struggle is but a phase of the logical development of our revolution; it is the struggle of a poor but large people against those that starve others and fiercely hold the monopoly of all the wealth and of all the gold of the world; it is the struggle of a fertile and young people against those that have lost their fecundity and face their sunset; it is the struggle between two centuries and two ideas.

Now that the dice have been cast and our will has burned the ships behind us, I solemnly declare that Italy does not intend to drag into the conflict other nations with which she shares sea or land borders. Switzerland, Yugoslavia, Greece, Turkey, and Egypt should take note of these words of mine. It depends on them, and only on them, whether or not they will be rigorously confirmed.

Italians!

In a memorable gathering, the one in Berlin, I said that, according to the laws of fascist morality, when one has a friend, one marches with him to the end. ("Duce! Duce! Duce!"). This we have done and this we shall do with Germany, with her people, and with her wonderful armed forces.

On this eve of an event that will reach through the centuries, we turn our thoughts to His Majesty the King Emperor (the crowd erupts into cheers for the House of Savoy), who, as always, has interpreted the soul of the nation. And we salute the Führer, leader of the great allied Germany (the people cheers at length for Hitler).

Italy, proletarian and Fascist, is for the third time standing, strong, proud, and united as never before (the crowd screams with one voice: "Yes!"). There exists only one word categorical and binding for everyone. It already flies across and inflames the hearts from the Alps to the Indian Ocean: Victory! (The people burst forth in high acclaim). And we will win, to finally give a long period of peace and justice to Italy, to Europe, and to the world.

Italian People! Run to the arms and demonstrate your tenacity, your courage, and your valour!

The following article is reproduced from the digitised original, which is available on the web site of the National Library of Australia. For the full speech, refer to Appendix C.

MUSSOLINI PROCLAIMS ITALY AN EMPIRE

Sovereignty Over Abyssinia

KING VICTOR EMMANUEL EMPEROR

Thousands Cheer Duce's Pronouncement

LONDON, May 10.

Signor Mussolini announced last night that Ethiopia had been placed under the full and entire sovereignty of Italy. He proclaimed the King of Italy Emperor of Abyssinia. Marshal Badoglio will be viceroy.

Four hundred thousand people who had assembled before the Palazza Venezia cheered wildly when the Duce made the announcement. Rejoicings were continued until the early hours of this morning.

"Ethiopia's destiny is sealed," Signor Mussolini declared. "All knots have been severed by our shining sword. Italy, at last, has her Empire."

Signor Mussolini's pronouncement was preceded by a characteristically brief meeting of the Fascist Grand Council. The meeting, which began at 10 p.m., lasted 10 minutes. Signor Mussolini then summoned the Cabinet, which sat for three minutes to confirm the most momentous decision in the history of modern Italy.

Signor Mussolini at 10.30 p.m. ap- peared on the famous balcony from which he has made so many speeches, and was received with thunderous acclamation.

Great Event Accomplished

Signor Mussolini said:–

"Officers, non-commissioned officers, men of all the armed forces in Africa and Italy, Blackshirts of the revolution, and Italian men and women at home and throughout the world, hearken! With the decision which the Grand Council has approved a great event is accomplished. Ethiopia's destiny is sealed to-day–May 9, in the fourteenth year of the Fascist era.

EMPEROR OF ABYSSINIA

"All knots have been severed by our shining sword. The African victory re- mains in the hlstory of our country, complete and pure, like the legionaries who have fallen desired it to be.

"Italy al last last her Empire – that Fascist Empire which bears the imperishable signs of truth and the power of Rome's emblem. It is an Empire of peace, because Italy wants pence for herself and for all.

"This is the goal for which, for 14 years, the eruptive energies of the young Italian generation have been disciplined, and at which the energies of future generations will be directed. Italy wars only when she is compelled to do bo by the needs of existence.

"The territories of the peoples belonging to the Empire of Abyssinia will be placed under the full and entire sove- reignty of Italy: the King will assume the title of Emperor for himself and his successors.

Empire on Hills of Rome

"The people of Italy created the Empire with their blood, they will moke it fruitful by labour, and defend it against anyone. In this supreme certainty, leglonaries raise your banners, your steel, your hearts to salute after 15 centuries, the reappearance of an Empire on the hills of Rome. Will you bo worthy of it?"

Slgnor Mussolini paused and there was a united shout of "Si si"

"This cry," he added, "resembles a sacred oath, binding you before God and men for life and death. Blackshirts and legionaries, salute your King."

The Governor of Lybia (Air-Marshal Balbo), Marshal Debono (formerly Commander in Chief in East Africa), and other Fascist veterans crowded round Signor Mussolini and kissed him as he left the balcony. Guns began to fire salvoes and Signor Mussolini had to reappear on the balcony nine times bcfore the cheering crowds would disperse. The roar of the cheering

Captive Down Under

was so great that it drowned the reverberations of the artillery salute of 21 guns to the new Emperor and the Italian triumph.

A message from Geneva states that Italy's proclamation of the foundation of an Empire is regarded not only as a challenge to the League, but to the United States and the South American republics, which signed a pact that they would not recognise the puppet State of Manchoukuo. It Is not expected that they will recognise an Italianised Abyssinia.

General Graziani who played a leading part in the campaign against the Abyssinians, and who, it was reported at one time, would be appointed Governor of Addis Ababa, has been created a marshal.

The former Crown Prince Wilhelm of Germany has sent a telegram to Signor Mussolini reading: –

"Congratulations upon your victory in war, which, notwithstanding all opposition, you have brought to a conclusion to the surprise of everyone."

Cheering Thousands

The crowds began to assemble long before Signor Mussolini appeared. The Piazza Venezia and surrounding streets for a radius of half a mile were packed with solid masses of people excitedly awaiting the announcement of the crea- tion of the new Roman Empire.

As night fell hundreds of electric bulbs illuminated the hlstoric buildings, from every window of which hung a tricolour. Torches flared and naval searchlights floodlit banners inscribcd with patriotic slogans.

Twenty thousand soldiers, sailors, marines, and airman, accoutred as for war, with every tenth man holding a blazing torch, lined the steps of the massive Victor Emmanuel monument, the Imperial Way, and the boulevards facing the Capitol, forming a gigantic guard of honour for the Duce. Massed bands played Fascist hymns and church bells pealed. All over the country millions were demon- strating theil joy at the victory.

When Signor Mussolini walked on to the balcony lie was accompanied by members of the Fasclst Grand Council and Am- bassadors and Ministers of nations which had not imposed sanctions.

As Signor Mussolini advanced the tumultuous cheering rose to a crescendo of delirious joy. A fanfare of trumpets commanded silence, but the Duce's speech was punctuated by cheers and applause.

After Signor Mussolini's address a decree was published formally proclaiming Italian sovereignty over Abyssinia, vesting the King with the title of Emperor of Abyssinia and Marshal Badoglio with that or Viceroy. All the decisions will become effective immedlately.

The Fascist Grand Council passed a resolution expressing the country's grati- tude to the Duce as the founder of the Empire.

UNCOMPROMISING SPEECH

No Reference to Other Nations Rome, May 10.

Signor Mussolini's speech was absolutely uncompromising. It proclaimed a situation, which, it is declared, here, is unalterable, unless Europe goes to war against Italy. The speech did not contain any reference to foreign nations or their Interests in Abyssinia.

CREATED VICEROY

The proclamation In the "Rome Gazette" begins: "The territories and peoples for- merly belonging lo the Emperor of Abyssinia are placed under the full and entire sovereignty of the Kingdom of Italy and the title of Emperor of Italy is assumed by the King or Italy for himself and his successors."

Thus a concrete fact confronts the Council of the League, whose future actions must be decided In the light of Signor Mussolini's declaration that Italy will de- fend her conquest with arms. The League may decline to recognise the annexation, but the view is expressed that it will be powerless to prevent Italy's exploitation of Abyssinia's resources.

After he had delivered his speech Signor Mussolini received the Ambassadors and Ministers of countries that had not im- posed sanctions. Later he conferred with the Italian Ambassador to Great Britain (Signor Grandi), who then left for London. The newspapers issued special midnight editions with headlines 61n. in height.

Appendix C
Proclamation of the Empire, Rome 9 May 1936

This is Mussolini's speech to proclaim the Italian Empire. The original recording is available on YouTube. I have omitted the repeated cheering of the crowd, which interrupted the speech eighteen times. Mussolini only spoke when the whole audience was completely quiet.

Comrades, salute the Duce! (1)

Officers! Non-commissioned officers! Soldiers of all the national armed forces in Africa and Italy! Blackshirts of the revolution! Italian men and women at home and throughout the world! Hearken! With the decisions that you will know in few moments and that were acclaimed by the Grand Council of Fascism, a great event is being accomplished: Ethiopia's destiny is sealed, today, the 9th of May, fourteenth year of the Fascist Era. (2)

All knots were severed by our shining sword, and the African victory remains in the history of our fatherland whole and pure, like the fallen and surviving legionaries dreamed and desired it to be.

Italy has at last her Empire. A Fascist Empire, because it bears the indestructible signs of will and power of the Roman fasces and because this is the goal for which for fourteen years the bursting and disciplined energies of the young and vigorous Italian generations were urged. An Empire of peace, because Italy wants peace for herself and for all and only decides to go to war when she is compelled to do so by imperious, incoercible needs of existence. An Empire of civilisation and humanity for all peoples of Ethiopia. This is in the tradition of Rome, which, after having won, associated the peoples to its destiny.

Here is the law, Italians, that closes a period of our history and opens another like an immense passage to all possibilities for the future:

1. *The territories and the people that belonged to the Empire of Ethiopia are placed under the full and complete sovereignty of the Kingdom of Italy.*

2. *The title of Emperor is... The title of Emperor is assumed by the King of Italy for himself and his successors.*

Officers! Non-commissioned officers! Soldiers of all the national armed forces in Africa and Italy! Blackshirts! Italian men and women! The Italian people have created the Empire with their blood. They will fertilise it with their work and defend it with their weapons against anyone. In this supreme certainty, legionaries, raise your banners, your steel, and your hearts to salute after fifteen centuries, the reappearance of the Empire on the fateful hills of Rome.

Will you be worthy of it? (The crowd erupts into a formidable "Si!")

This cry is like a sacred oath, which binds you before God and men for life and death!

Blackshirts! Legionaries! Salute the King!

1. I used here the words "comrade" to translate the Italian word "camerata" because there is no exact English equivalent. "Comrade" is also how Communists and Socialists refer to one another in English. In Italian, Communists called one another "compagno", which is the Italian word for "mate" or "partner". Fascists were very militaristic, and "camerata" is the Italian word to indicate a dormitory in a barrack.

2. Italian Fascism (i.e., the original and quintessential Fascism, the Fascism by definition) remained in power from 1922 to 1945. The Fascist Era (or EF for *Era Fascista*) referred to the numbering of years beginning from 1922, when Mussolini marched on Rome and compelled the King to give him control of the government. Therefore, EF XIV was the year 1936.

Captive Down Under

Appendix D
List of PWCC from the AWM

I reproduced the following table from the typewritten original (AWM Volume 1, Part 3, Chapter 1 – Accomodation for P.W. and Internees, pp 236-237).

SCHEDULE OF 96 PW CONTROL CENTRES IN AUSTRALIA – 1943-1946

FROM WHICH PW WERE EMPLOYED ON FARMS

STATE	LOCATION	APPROX NO. OF PW	PERIOD OF OPERATION	
			FROM	TO
Queensland	GAYNDAH	150	Dec 43	Dec 45
	KINGAROY	150	May 44	Dec 45
	MONTO	150	May 44	Dec 45
	NAMBOUR	200	Dec 43	Jan 46
	GYMPIE	200	Dec 43	Jan 46
	KENILWORTH	150	Apr 44	Jan 46
	STANTHORPE	200	Sep 43	Feb 46
	BOONAH	100	May 44	Feb 46
	ATHERTON	60	Jul 45	Sep 45
New South Wales	COONABARABRAN	151	Jun 43	Jan 46
	PARKES	150	Jul 43	Jan 46
	ARMIDALE	226	Aug 43	Dec 45
	CANOWINDRA	121	Sep 43	Jan 46
	DORRIGO	121	Sep 43	Nov 45
	WAGGA	170	Oct 43	Jan 46
	ORANGE	164	Oct 43	Nov 45
	OBERON	133	Oct 43	Dec 45
	TAMWORTH	114	Nov 43	Dec 45
	GLEN INNES	100	Dec 43	Dec 45
	MACKSVILLE	130	Nov 44	Nov 45
	MOSS VALE	110	Mar 44	Nov 45
	YOUNG	52	Mar 44	Nov 45
	TUMUT	51	Mar 44	Nov 45

	MUDGEE	80	Mar 44	Dec 45
	WELLINGTON	91	Mar 44	Jan 46
	TEMORA	90	Mar 44	Jan 46
	INVERNELL	52	Mar 44	Dec 45
	MURWILLUMBAH	196	Apr 44	Nov 45
	QUIRINDI	60	Apr 44	Jan 45
	WEST WYALONG	57	Apr 44	Jan 46
	DUNEDOO	80	May 44	Jan 46
	LISMORE	206	Jun 44	Nov 45
	KYOGLE	97	Jun 44	Dec 46
	TAREE	99	May 44	Nov 45
	GUNNEDAH	75	Jun 44	Jan 46
	NARROMINE	88	Jun 44	Jan 46
Victoria *and* *Riverina*	HAMILTON	200	Jun 43	Mar 46
	COLAC	200	Jun 43	Mar 46
	LEONGATHA	200	Aug 43	Apr 46
	FOSTER	120	Jun 45	Apr 46
	KYNETON	225	Sep 43	Feb 46
	YARRAH	210	Mar 44	Mar 46
	WANGARATTA	175	Mar 44	Deb 46
	BERRIGAN	150	Feb 44	Jan 46
	HENTY	100	Feb 44	Jan 46
	WARRAGUL	225	Mar 44	Apr 46
	MAFFRA	180	Mar 44	Mar 46
	CAMPERDOWN	150	Mar 44	Feb 46
	KERANG	120	Jun 44	Apr 46
	SWANN HILL	100	May 44	Mar 46
	YEA	100	Aug 45	Feb 46
	CORRYONG	25	Jul 44	Mar 46
South Australia	MT BARKER-WOODSIDE	150	Oct 43	Mar 46
	WILLUNGA	175	Dec 43	Mar 46
	CLARE	195	Feb 44	Mar 46
	MURRAY BRIDGE	160	Feb 44	Mar 46
	MT GAMBIER	85	Feb 44	Mar 46
	MT PLEASANT	100	Apr 44	Nov 45
	NARACOORTE	150	May 44	Mar 46
	LAMEROO	100	May 44	Mar 46

	BORDERTOWN	90	Jul 44	Nov 45
	MAITLAND	95	Jul 44	Mar 46
	TUMBY BAY	150	Feb 45	Mar 46
Western Australia	BRIDGETOWN	175	Oct 43	May 46
	KENDENUP	150	Nov 43	May 46
	DARKAN	100	Nov 43	Oct 45
	KOJUNUP	150	Mar 44	May 46
	TAMBELLUP	125	Mar 44	May 46
	WAGIN	175	Mar 44	May 46
	POPANYINNING	125	Mar 44	May 46
	MARGARET RIVER	150	Mar 44	May 46
	BEVERLEY	125	Apr 44	May 46
	QUAIRADING	125	Apr 44	May 46
	KELLERBERRIN	175	Apr 44	May 46
	NAREMBEEN	150	May 44	May 46
	KUNUNOPPIN	125	Jun 44	May 46
	KUKERIN	125	Jun 44	May 46
	YEALERING	125	Jun 44	Oct 45
	WYALKATCHEM	100	Jun 44	Mar 46
	KONDININ	150	Jun 44	May 46
	NEWDEGATE	100	Jun 44	May 46
	KOORDA	125	Jul 44	May 46
	BUNBURY	100	Mar 45	May 46
	TOODYAY	125	Mar 45	May 46
	WONGAN HILLS	125	Mar 45	May 46
	DALWALLINU	175	Mar 45	May 46
	MOORA	125	Apr 45	May 46
	THREE SPRINGS	150	Apr 45	May 46
	MULLEWA	100	May 45	May 46
Tasmania	BURNIE	382	Nov 43	Mar 46
	SCOTTSDALE	213	Jan 44	Mar 46
	HOBART	212	Feb 44	Mar 46
	SMITHTON	166	Jun 44	Mar 46
	DELORAINE	179	Jun 44	Mar 46
	CONARA	97	Aug 44	Mar 46
	HUONVILLE	89	Jun 45	Aug 45

Appendix E
Sending a letter to a prisoner in Australia

The Australian War Memorial has in its archives the envelope of a letter sent to Lt. Bellotti Bon, an Italian POW held in Australia. It shows that it was censored three times: by the Italians, by the Americans, and by the Australians. The stamps were removed to check that no text was hidden underneath.

The letter was sent from Genova on 5 September 1942 to Murchison camp and was received in Myrtleford camp on 3 January 1943, four months later. If you look at the Service and Casualty form of Lieutenant Bellotti Bon available for download from the NAA's web site (Service and Casualty Form for prisoner PWI47075, NAA, series MP1103/1), you will see that when the letter arrived at Murchison, the prisoner had already been in Myrtleford for three months. This gives you an idea of the limited possibilities the POWs had to communicate with their families. (1)

But Lt Bellotti Bon was among the lucky ones: he was repatriated in August 1945, almost one and a half years before most of the other prisoners.

1. A report by the Army Headquarters (AWM) provides the list of all POW camps built in Australia. Wikipedia provides a streamlined version of the list but adds some transit and temporary camps (unverified) (List_of_World_War_II_prisoner-of-war_camps_in_Australia, accessed on 2021-04-20).

Appendix F
Hay POW Camp 7

The following image is reproduced from Haywire (Hay Historical Society).

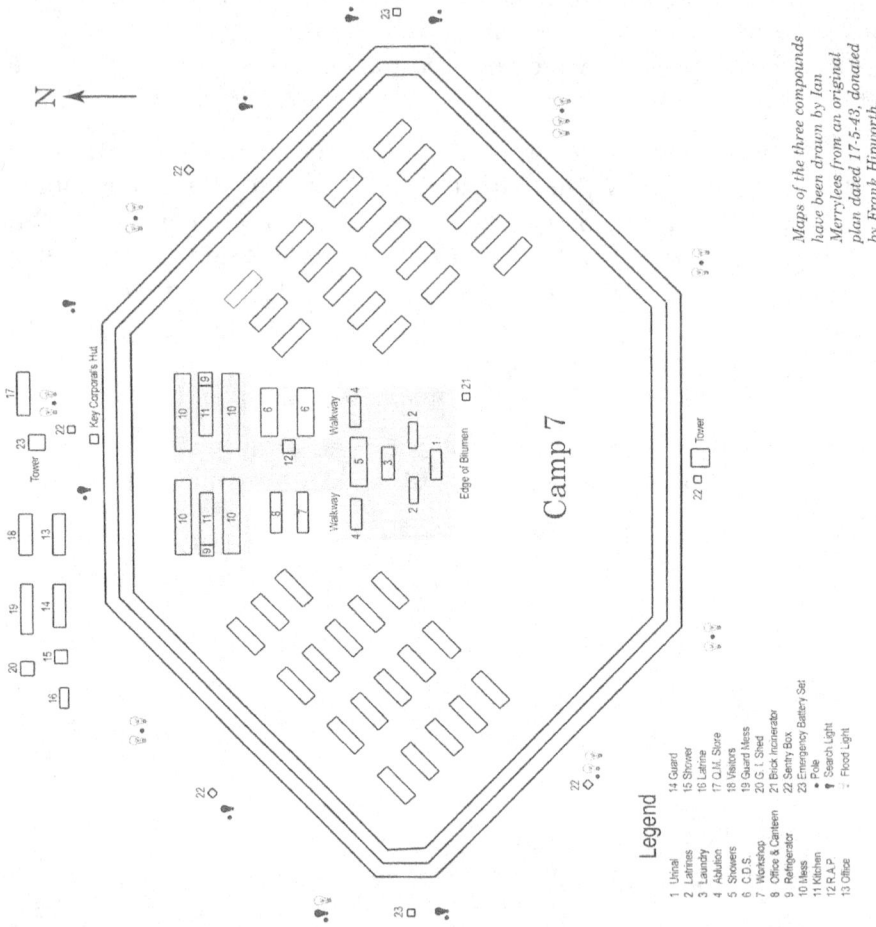

For those unfamiliar with military abbreviations, CDS means "Camp Dressing Station", while RAP means "Regimental Aid Post" (an infirmary).

I obtained the following image from Flinders University. It is a reproduction of the map drawn by Luigi Bortolotti in his diary.

Bortolotti's version of the map shows a football field and the hut numbering, which are missing from the Haywire map. Bortolotti also explains that the hut marked N on his map (adjacent to hut number 14) was used as a workshop.

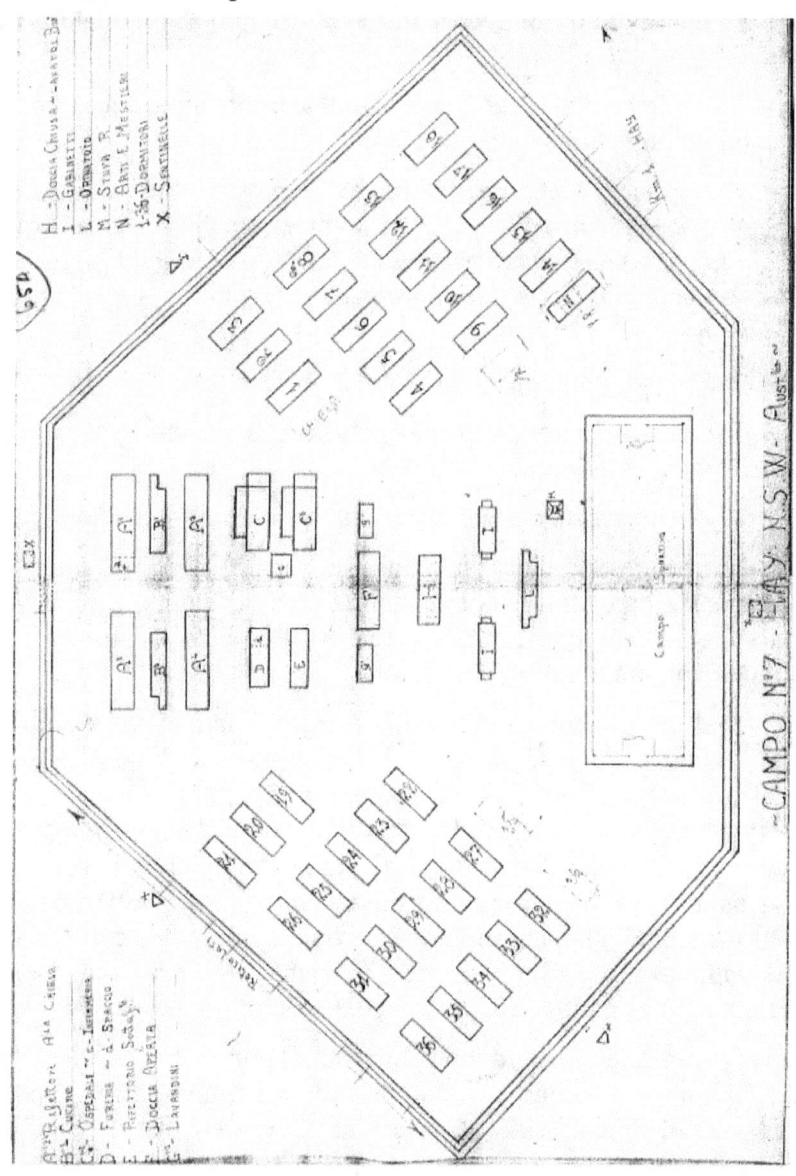

Appendix G
Badoglio's Proclamation

Pietro Badoglio was the general of the Italian Army that the Italian King Victor Emmanuel III nominated as prime minister on 25 July 1943, after dismissing Mussolini.

At 19:45 of 8 September 1943, he made a radio announcement that translated into English as follows:

> *The Italian government, recognising the impossibility of continuing the unequal struggle against an overwhelming enemy force, in order to avoid further and graver disasters for the Nation, sought an armistice from general Eisenhower, commander-in-chief of the Anglo-American Allied forces.*
>
> *The request was granted.*
>
> *Consequently, all acts of hostility against the Anglo-American forces by Italian forces must cease everywhere.*
>
> *But they may react to possible attacks from any other source.*

Eisenhower had forced Badoglio's hand in making the proclamation by announcing the capitulation of Italy on the BBC earlier in the afternoon of the 8th. The Italians had repeatedly asked the allies to postponed the announcement, but to no avail.

It can be speculated that with "any other source" Badoglio referred to the Germans, who, under the command of Generalfeldmarschall (Field Marshal) Albert Kesselring, had been concentrating troops in Italy precisely in preparation of an expected defection of Italy from the Axis (the alliance between Germany, Italy, and Japan). But he didn't spell it out. This was not just an announcement made to the Italian people. It also was what the Italian commanders throughout the Mediterranean had to work with, as they didn't receive any specific order from the "Supreme Commander" (i.e., Badoglio). What were they supposed to do?

Some sea commanders sailed their ships out of port and escaped to Spain. Others fought the Germans, while still others surrendered to them. On land or at sea, the result was the same: many lives were lost.

Captive Down Under

Meanwhile, the King, who still in the morning of the 8th had reassured the German Ambassador in Rome of Italy's loyalty, escaped to a harbour on the east coast of Italy and from there to the southern city of Brindisi, where Badoglio established a government in exile. No wonder that the Germans called Italy's separate peace a betrayal and, perhaps, no wonder that less than three years later the Italians chose to make Italy a republic and banned all male members of the royal familty from ever re-entering the country.

Appendix H
Allies but still Prisoners

When on October 13th 1943 Italy declared war on Germany and joined the battle on the side of the Allies, it seemed impossible for the allies to keep in captivity citizens of what had become a co-belligerent nation. On the other hand, the British didn't want to have thousands of uncontrollable young men loose in their countries. Additionally, there were not enough officers or suitable linguists capable of leading units formed out of Italian soldiers currently in captivity and, in any case, neither British nor Italian officers would have had the legal rights to enforce discipline on such units.

The British considered the possibility of enrolling the Italian prisoners into the regular British army, but then, they would have had to treat the new recruits like every other British soldier, and that was considered to be unacceptable by the British authorities.

Moreover, and perhaps compellingly, Italian POWs in British hands were supporting the war effort with their work in factories and farms. Such schemes could be expanded to include many, if not all, of the 250,000 prisoners held throughout the Empire. Why waste such a resource? On the subject of its prisoners and their status, employment, and repatriation, Italy never took a clear and firm stand, thereby letting the British interpret Badoglio's position as they saw fit.

Pressed by their British allies, the Americans reluctantly agreed that the Italian soldiers held by the British keep their POW status, a situation that in Australia was going to be maintained till the beginning of 1947.

The misfortune for many Italian POWs was to have been captured too early, and to have become too useful to an Allied war effort which was constantly short of manpower and willing to extend to the limit the boundaries of international treaties in order to make use of all available resources.

Abbreviations

AB   Able Seaman

ACT   Australian Capital Territory

AD   Anno Domini (*Year of the Lord* in Latin)

AM   Ante Meridiem, which means before noon in Latin

ANZAC   Australian and New Zealand Army Corps

AWM   Australian War Memorial

BBC   British Broadcasting Corporation

BC   Before Christ

BCE   Before the Common Era

CC   Control Centre

CDS   Camp Dressing Station

CE   Common Era. It replaces the confessional abbreviation AD. Similarly, BCE replaces BC.

CRS   Commonwealth Record Series

DO   Dominions Office

EF   *Era Fascista* (Fascist Era).

GHCN   Global Historical Climatology Network

H.M.S.   His/Her Majesty Ship, a vessel belonging to the British Royal Navy.

ICRC   International Committee of the Red Cross

ISBN   International Standard Serial Number. It uniquely identifies periodicals.

JAMA   Journal of the American Medical Association

NAA   National Archives of Australia

NLA   National Library of Australia

NOAA   National Oceanic and Atmospheric Administration

NSW	New South Wales
NT	Northern Territory
OK	Wikipedia lists dozens possible etymologies of OK4.
PM	Prime Minister
PNF	*Partito Nazionale Fascista* (Fascist National Party).
POW	Prisoner of War
PW	Prisoners of War
PW&I	Directorate of Prisoners of War and Internees at Army Headquarters
PWCC	Prisoner of War Control Centre
PWI	Prisoner of War from Italy: one of the codes included in the POW identification codes.
RAP	Regimental Aid Post
RIA	Royal Italian Army
RIN	Royal Italian Navy
S.S.	Screw Steamer
SS	Schutzstaffel, which in English means Protection/Defence Squadron/Corps.
TNG	Star Trek - The Next Generation series.
UK	United Kingdom
USA	United States of America
WA	Western Australia
WHO	World Health Organisation
WS	Western Australia
WWI	Word War I
WWII	The second world war, generally considered to span the six years between the German invasion of Poland on 1 September 1939 and the formal surrender of Japan on 2 September 1945